She opened her eyes to see Wolfe quietly watching her. Nichelle was overcome by a nearly overwhelming desire to touch him. It would be so easy to crawl down to the other end of the couch and bite, kiss and lick every inch of bare flesh.

"It's beautiful, isn't it?" His gaze did not leave hers.

She could only nod, swallowing heavily as the sweet and thick need rolled through her veins.

"I've wanted to come to Marrakesh since I was a kid," Wolfe said softly.

"Why didn't you?" Nichelle tucked her hip deeper into the couch, trying to put some space between their bodies. But Wolfe's sock-clad foot followed her skin, tucking into her with a slight and suggestive caress. Was he doing this to her on purpose?

Wolfe shrugged. "Work became more important to me than seeing the world."

"I never thought I'd hear you say work became more important than enjoying life," she murmured.

They were caught in a delicate cocoon together, lulled into a gentle world made simply of their own voices, the lush beauty of the room, the faint smell of Moroccan amber that billowed up from the couch like fine smoke. It felt like blasphemy to speak above a whisper.

Dear Reader,

Wolfe Diallo is a man of sin and selfishness, at least that's what he thinks. His mother cheated on his father when he was young, leaving Wolfe mistrustful of long-term intimacy and of his own genetic predisposition to take rather than to give.

Nichelle Wright is a good girl, despite her love of designer stilettos and premium vodka. After all, for most of her life she's ignored that tasty morsel, Wolfe Diallo, who had been dangling under her nose the whole time. Now, after a long look at what he has to offer, she wants to ditch her good-girl ways for a taste of what she suddenly craves.

Find out with me, dear reader, if Wolfe's sin and Nichelle's sweetness will end up being an explosive mix.

Decadently yours,

Lindsay Evans

AFFAIR OF *Pleasure*

Recycling programs
for this product may
not exist in your area.

ISBN-13: 978-0-373-86420-1

Affair of Pleasure

Copyright © 2015 by Lindsay Evans

HARLEQUIN®
www.Harlequin.com

Printed in U.S.A.

Lindsay Evans was born in Jamaica and currently lives and writes in Atlanta, Georgia, where she's constantly on the hunt for inspiration, club in hand. She loves good food and romance and would happily travel to the ends of the earth for both. Find out more at lindsayevanswrites.com.

Books by Lindsay Evans

Harlequin Kimani Romance

Pleasure Under the Sun
Sultry Pleasure
Snowy Mountain Nights
Affair of Pleasure

Visit the Author Profile page at Harlequin.com for more titles.

To my readers, old and new.
Thank you for sharing your time with me.

ACKNOWLEDGMENTS

This new journey of mine wouldn't be possible without
Sheree L. Greer, Angela Gabriel and Dorothy Lindsay.
As my beta reader, Sheree has read more romance novels
than she'd ever even thought possible,
and Angela has suffered with me through many
plotting sessions over dinner and ice cream.
Dorothy Lindsay has simply always been there.

Kimberly Kaye Terry, as ever, thank you.

Chapter 1

"Nichelle, wait!"

Nichelle Wright turned at the sound of her name, pivoting on the heels of her teal Louboutin stilettos. "What can I help you with, Steve?"

Steve Brooks stood in the middle of the well-lit hallway of Kingston Consulting with his shirtsleeves rolled up and his tie loosened, although it was just past ten in the morning. He shoved his hands in his pockets and relaxed his stance, as if he had all day to waste Nichelle's time.

She tapped the manila folder she carried against her thigh and quirked an eyebrow, wordlessly telling him to hurry it along.

Steve finally started talking. "About the Trestle presentation you did this morning, Nichelle. Can you break something else down for me…?"

Nichelle heard a door click open behind her, far enough away that she knew it was her business partner's office at the end of the hallway. She'd always teased him that for someone who was so friendly and sociable, he was giving mixed signals by taking the office farthest from everyone. Hers was at the opposite end of the hall, in the thick of things.

She glanced over her shoulder. Wolfe Diallo stood in the doorway, getting ready to walk a woman toward the elevators. He was dressed for a day of meetings, his solid six and a half feet clad in a gray three-piece suit. His head looked freshly shaved, and the goatee framing his mouth was crisp and on point, as always. He was a model businessman. Emphasis on *model*. His gorgeous looks made the men between the covers of *Vogue Hommes International* look like toothless hobos.

The woman with him wasn't dressed for business, though. Her voluptuous frame was on display in a tight white dress and red screw-me pumps that gleamed with a suggestive, wet shine. Nichelle's lips twitched.

She caught Wolfe's eye as he walked toward her with the woman by his side. Nichelle tipped her head toward his now closed office door. He paused and said something to the woman, brushed her cheek with his and gave her a brilliant smile. A dismissal. The woman's own smile dimmed, but she still looked up at Wolfe with a mixture of hunger and aloofness. *Come get me but don't think I'm needy.* A true talent.

"Excuse me, Steve." Nichelle returned her full attention to him. "Come to my office a little later if you want to talk more about the project. I'll be around." She met his eyes, daring him to push forward with his obvious delaying tactic. "Okay?"

"Sure." He looked briefly panicked, darting his gaze to the woman with Wolfe.

Nichelle dismissed him and headed down the hallway. As she passed the woman, she nodded, but only got a cold look in return. She felt more than saw the wide doe eyes flickering over her uniform, or what she considered her uniform—white blouse and calf-length black pencil skirt. Her green heels matched her optimistic and peaceful mood.

"Good morning, Wolfe." She walked into the office past him, her shoulder brushing the lapel of his pewter Zegna suit.

The office was cozy and warm, like his den at home, decorated with imported rugs and rust-colored walls. A large painting of Vermont in autumn dominated one wall. On his bookshelf rested a black Bose speaker dock and matching iPod. Next to them sat a vase of irises, Nichelle's favorite flowers that Wolfe's assistant replaced every few days.

"Is it a good morning, or is it great?" He closed the door behind him with a warm chuckle.

The office smelled like the perfume of the woman who'd just left, something musky and warm. Not unpleasant. Nichelle perched her hip on the edge of the wide window in Wolfe's office and glanced down to the street eight stories below.

"For me, it's only a good one," she said. "But it will be even better once we get on the same page about this potential million-dollar contract." She dropped her manila folder and a thumb drive on his desk then went back to her window perch.

Instantly, Wolfe's stance was all business—his smile

more predatory, the velvet eyes hardened to something like steel. He sat behind his desk. "Tell me more."

She started in on her mini presentation. Once she finished giving him the details of her latest project, a client she planned to go after for their management consulting firm, he grinned with all his teeth. Like a shark on the scent of fresh blood.

"Yes," he said. "You know I want it."

"Good." She crossed her legs and glanced down briefly at the long line of her calf, the arch of her feet dipping into the five-inch stilettos. "The thumb drive has everything I've prepared, including the actual proposal. Once you've looked it over—*today* would be lovely—" She flashed him her own toothy smile. "—I'll put in our bid. There are a few others I have in mind, but this is the biggest and the one we need to focus on for now. We're ready to grow and grow big."

"I agree," Wolfe said. "I trust you. That's one of the main reasons I asked you to come work with me."

Nichelle's lips curled in amusement. He hadn't really asked but rather *seduced* her into coming to work with him when he'd decided to leave the family business in favor of striking out on his own. Their families had been friends and neighbors for years, but instead of approaching her like a friend, he made her a business proposition. At first, he asked her to come on as a junior partner, someone to spot trends, grow and shape the management consulting firm in a way that made them money but also positioned them in the most advantageous way possible in the market. But she knew her worth and refused his initial offer.

At Sterling Solutions, the firm he'd hired her away from, her success rate was damned near legendary. Sterling had been on the verge of offering her more—a bigger office, possibly even a full partnership. Somehow Wolfe found out and raised the dollar amount and incentives with his offer. When she refused him again, he laid out the ultimate prize of an equal partnership at Kingston Consulting, plus an indecently large signing bonus.

"I'm just giving you your money's worth," Nichelle said with a pointed smile.

They both knew he'd made back the money he invested in bringing her on within the first quarter and tripled it by the second. So far, three years later, they were both very happy with the arrangement.

"And speaking of which." She dipped a shoulder toward the door. "We might need to fire Steve Brooks."

Wolfe leaned back in his chair and watched her over steepled fingers. "Of course, if you think it's necessary. Care to let me know why?"

She shook her head, almost amused but not quite. "He was trying to stop me from coming into your office and seeing you with your latest...female companion."

"Oh, yeah?"

There was a persistent rumor around the office that Nichelle and Wolfe were more than business partners. Even after three years of seeing nothing more intimate between them than shared laughter and a few platonic touches, nearly everyone at Kingston Consulting was still convinced they were sleeping together.

"I think under the man code, he was trying to protect you from being caught with another woman right under my naïve and unsuspecting nose."

They exchanged crooked smiles at the thought of her being naïve or gullible enough not to know what Wolfe was up to with his myriad and varied lady friends. "He was being deceptive," she said.

"Depends on how you look at it." Wolfe grinned at her from across the desk. "Another CEO would give him a promotion."

She waved a hand in dismissal. They both knew what kind of CEO Wolfe was. "The corporate version of 'bros before hos'?" she murmured.

"That fool is no bro of mine."

"You should probably let him know that."

It was Wolfe's turn to be dismissive. Steve Brooks wasn't important enough to warrant that sort of conversation. He was a damned good software engineer, and that was the reason they both kept him around, despite his persistent attempts to date every woman in the building. The women saw him as mostly harmless, but if Nichelle ever got an actual complaint about Brooks, he was out on his ass without discussion. No matter how good he was at his job.

Wolfe's cell phone buzzed, and he glanced down at it. "Don't forget about dinner at my parents' place on Friday evening." He tapped the phone to dismiss whatever he saw on the screen. "Mama wanted to make sure you're available and don't have to be off someplace saving the world."

"The only thing I'm out there saving on a regular basis is your ass." Nichelle smiled at the thought of his mother, a petite and fashionable fifty-something woman who'd given birth to thirteen energetic kids and somehow still had the time to successfully fulfill her role as chief operations officer at the family-run Diallo Corporation. "You know I'll be there." She pulled out her iPhone and checked the calendar to be sure. "It's already on the schedule."

"Nice to know we rate a slot in your precious schedule."

"Of course." With a gracious smile, she stood up from her improvised window seat. "You always do."

Wolfe came around his desk to walk her to the door. "By the way, I'll have Kathleen in HR draw up Brooks's dismissal letter today."

She paused in the doorway, her head tilted in consideration. "No, don't do that." After all, Steve Brooks had a sister he was helping put through college. He needed the money. "I'll keep an eye on him for now and let you know what happens."

He nodded. "Keep me in the loop."

"Of course." She walked out into the hall and headed to her own office, mind already on her next meeting. "Later alligator." The heels of her stilettos rang sharply against the hardwood floors with every step.

Wolfe very consciously closed his office door instead of watching Nichelle walk away. She was cripplingly beautiful. And those ridiculously sexy shoes she insisted on wearing every day never failed to stir his…interest.

He knew his feelings for her were inappropriate. She was his business partner, the person he trusted more than anyone else on earth. When he was eighteen, he took his father's half-million-dollar antique Bentley without permission. He drove it all over Miami and returned it with, unfortunately, a tiny scratch on the driver's side. His father was furious, demanding the one who stole the car to confess. Wolfe never did. The scar stayed on the car for months before his father eventually grew frustrated and fixed it himself. Nichelle saw Wolfe return the car, though. To this day, she never told a soul. After that, Wolfe trusted her with all his secrets, large and small. She hadn't disappointed him yet.

But in addition to being the keeper of his secrets, Nichelle was also the epitome of walking sex with a genius IQ and a sense of humor that never failed to make him laugh. He'd have to be made of stone not to notice and appreciate everything about her, and he was certainly *not* made of stone.

At his desk, he reopened the text reminder about dinner from his mother. As always, he felt that uncomfortable mix of love and resentment whenever she reached out to him. Each overture from her seemed like an attempt to make amends for that terrible thing she'd done to the family when Wolfe was sixteen years old.

He didn't trust her.

When he'd needed her the most, she'd packed her bags and left the family for another man, a successful painter who'd taken her away to Vanuatu. She was gone for nearly five months, having disappeared into a place Wolfe hadn't even heard of until his father announced a sudden trip there, then brought her back pregnant and far from penitent.

It was a lapse that no one in the family talked about, not even Wolfe's older brother, Kingsley, who must have noticed the same things Wolfe did. After his mother gave birth to her child—a child his father never treated any differently—she settled back into the routine of family life as if her five month defection had never happened.

But for Wolfe, it was the single most defining act of his childhood.

He swiped a finger across the phone screen and

brought up his mother's number, then sent her a text arranging for them to talk later that day. He was checking in on her. He knew it, and she did, too. It irritated him that after sixteen years, he still had the need to call her at least once a week to see where her head was. As if anything he could say would ever change her mind if she decided to leave the family again. Once she wanted something, there was no stopping her from getting it. That was one of the many things, unfortunately, that they had in common.

Wolfe glanced at the closed door of his office and remembered the sleek silhouette of Nichelle standing in the doorway. Her hourglass figure and sinful shoes. How she had sucked on the inside of her bottom lip as she considered the annoyance that was Steve Brooks.

Now *that*, he thought, was something he shouldn't want. But he did.

At the end of a long day, Nichelle was finally getting to the last pieces of mail in the secondary pile her assistant sorted for her every morning. It was mostly junk and solicitations addressed just to her. She fanned them out like a bad hand of poker and tipped them in the recycling, reject or respond pile as necessary. She frowned at an envelope from Sterling Solutions marked "private." There was nothing private she had to discuss with Teague Simonson, her former boss, or anyone else at Sterling. But her assistant, following protocol, hadn't opened the envelope. She tore it with her letter opener.

Nichelle,
It was a pleasure seeing you at the New York sustainability conference last month. I meant what I

*said about having a place for you to come back
to at Sterling. I see the stellar work you've done
with Kingston Solutions and want you to come
back and work that same magic for us. Nothing
less than full partnership and a corner office for
you, of course. Let's talk. I'll run some numbers
by you and see if we can't come to a mutually ben-
eficial arrangement.*

Teague

Nichelle tossed the letter in the recycle pile. She'd
already told Teague, at least half a dozen times, that
she wasn't interested in leaving Kingston. Now his unwanted communications were just obnoxious, no matter their tone. She wasn't going to respond to this latest
one. What was it about certain men that wouldn't let
them take no for an answer?

She sighed and glanced at her computer's clock. It
was nearly six. Wolfe had left the office an hour before
for a late meeting, and most of the staff was already
gone. Time for her to head out. Nichelle grabbed her
purse from its drawer and reached for her cell phone.
Her elbow knocked over the carefully sorted pile of
mail.

"Damn!" The letters slid halfway across her desk,
some falling on the floor. It was definitely time to go
home.

She haphazardly scooped the mail in a pile, determined to deal with it another day. Purse over her shoulder, she quickly left for the parking garage. In her car,
she turned on her favorite classic R&B station and eased
out into rush hour traffic. Seconds later, her phone rang.

Her sister's face showed up on the small screen. "Hey, Madalie."

"What are you up to?"

"Leaving work, which I'm sure you know."

Her sister giggled. "Yeah, I have you in the sights of my high-powered rifle now. I know exactly what you're doing." Madalie was currently indulging her obsession with spy novels and action movies. Everything was a gun or improbable martial arts metaphor.

"I'm at the beach kickin' it with some nice people. You should come."

Nichelle glanced from the slow traffic outside her window to her dashboard clock. "Do you have any idea what time it is?" It would take her at least forty minutes to get to the beach in that traffic.

"Of course. I was the one who called you after work, remember?"

Nichelle rolled her eyes. "Fine." Madalie had been floating her way through life for a few years now, twenty-four years old and still not knowing what she wanted to do for a career. She had her own place, her own money from the dividends of the stocks her father invested in her name. But her lack of direction and resulting listlessness worried Nichelle.

"Okay. I'll meet you there as soon as I can. You're at the usual place, right?"

"Of course. You know I don't handle change very well."

Half an hour later found Nichelle hiking across the sand with her high heels in hand. It was just past six thirty in the evening. The sky was hung with thick clouds while sunset burned its bright colors across the water. Her calf-length silk skirt and high-collared blouse weren't exactly made for the beach. The outfit was perfect for her perpetually air-conditioned office, but out here, she was more than a little warm. It didn't make sense for her to go home and change, though. For her sister, she'd endure a little discomfort.

The beach was surprisingly packed. She trudged across the sand, joining a broken line of people making their way to the oceanfront. It was a miracle she'd found parking. There was some sort of party going on. Bass-thumping dub-step music played from speakers set up around a high stage. Men and women, along with some teenagers, danced on the beach. She easily found her sister at the water's edge, her bright blue afro a beacon she followed to where Madalie sat at the edge of a bonfire, one of nearly a dozen or so people sitting in a circle, nodding along to the music and chatting.

"Hey! This party is great, right?" Madalie stood up to pull her into a hug.

"It's something." Nichelle glanced around her. "What's going on? It's a weekday. Shouldn't these people be in school or at work?"

"I think the work day is done." Madalie laughed. "Maybe I should have dragged Wolfe along to make sure you had a good time."

Nichelle ignored that comment. Still laughing, Madalie introduced her to the group gathered around the fire. Most nodded at her in acknowledgment before going back to their mostly silent enjoyment of the music. The smell of marijuana floated from somewhere nearby.

Scattered around on the sand were some blankets and a few folding chairs, abandoned while people danced to the throbbing music pouring out onto the beach. She considered grabbing one of the chairs, not in the mood to get sand and God knew what else on her black Balmain skirt. But at the knowing look from her sister, she dropped down into the sand. She only grumbled a little bit.

"Why did you drag me out here?"

"It's fun," Madalie said with a grin. "I invited Daddy and Willa, too. They're looking for parking now."

"Ah." After a moment's hesitation, Nichelle dropped her shoes at her side and leaned back in the sand. An impromptu family get together. She bumped Madalie's shoulder, and they shared a smile. "This is nice," Nichelle said. She worked so much that she didn't see her father or her two sisters as much as she'd like.

Madalie prowled the art district at all times of the day and night instead of focusing on her life's goals, while the youngest, Willa, was enrolled at the University of Miami, engrossed in her studies and enjoying being away from home. Nichelle barely knew what her father was up to. She didn't know when they had started to live their separate lives. After her mother died twenty years ago, the rest of the family stayed cooped up in the big Key Biscayne house together, none of them strong enough to go out into the world. But somehow, over time, things changed. Nichelle stopped feeling as if she was the only one holding her family together. Her sisters stopped expecting her to play the mother role. Her father started dating again. She'd gotten her life back enough to go off to California for college and then work. And though she didn't realize when exactly the transition happened, she jealously guarded the freedom she had now.

"You want some of this?" A shirtless man stumbled from his shuffling dance around the fire to offer Nichelle a blunt.

She shook her head in refusal. "Thank you, though."

He passed it on to someone else with a happy smile.

"This is what you invited Dad to?"

Madalie groaned and rolled her eyes. "Dad was young once, Nicki. He doesn't have a stick up his butt about stuff like this."

True enough. Their father was firmly of the carpe diem school of life. Grab it now since tomorrow is promised to no one.

"Still, it just seems wrong. If I were into this—" she gestured to the blunt being passed around the fire "—I don't know if I could smoke with him sitting right there."

"You're so uptight. Wolfe is definitely your more fun half." Madalie glanced over Nichelle's shoulder, and her eyes lit up. "Daddy! Willa!" She jumped to her feet and waved frantically at the two figures making their way through the growing crowd. They waved back.

Their father—serious in his Miami Dolphins cap and Wayfarer sunglasses—walked next to Willa, who kicked her way through the sand on bare feet, hands shoved in the pockets of her incredibly short shorts. Their father also wore shorts.

Nichelle greeted their father with a hug. "Hi, Dad." The last time she'd seen him, he was sitting at an outdoor café with a woman young enough to be one of his daughters. Nichelle had driven past the café, barely believing her eyes. But from that brief glimpse, he'd seemed happy.

"I thought you'd be too busy at the office to come

out this evening," he said to Nichelle, then kissed Madalie's forehead.

"Woman cannot live by massive paychecks alone," Nichelle said with a teasing smile.

He chuckled and sat next to her in the sand. "My baby is growing up."

Willa, the image of their long-dead mother with her stripper's body and angel face, smirked at Nichelle. "Yeah, I thought you'd be too tied up in the office with Wolfe to come out and play with us mere mortals."

Madalie snickered. "I wish it was bondage with that hot man instead of work that kept her in the office all day and night. It would at least be more interesting."

"And way more fun." Willa hiccupped with laughter.

"Screw you." Nichelle flipped off both her sisters. She was so tired of them harping on the imagined relationship between her and Wolfe. When it came from anyone else, she didn't care. But there was something about the way her sisters teased that always rubbed her raw.

Their father made a token sound of peacckccping. "Girls…"

"Okay, Daddy." The three chorused voices set off a round of laughter on the beach.

Fire crackled and sparked in the circle of stones, its light appearing brighter as the sun dimmed and dusk's softening colors spread across the horizon and over the ocean.

Nichelle leaned into her father's shoulder to watch the fire. *This*, she thought with a sigh, *feels perfect*. After a long day of conferences, meetings and negotiations, it felt good to simply *be*. No stress or expectations.

On the other side of their father, Madalie was asking Willa where she got her shorts. Nichelle hugged her knees to her chest and tilted her head up to the stars.

Chapter 2

"Pass me the rice and peas, Cheryl." Glendon Diallo reached out to his daughter for the white serving platter piled high with the fragrant dish.

The entire Diallo family, along with Nichelle and the rest of the Wrights, sat at the large oval table in the Diallos' dining room. Nineteen people, voices all raised in conversation and laughter. Hyacinth Diallo insisted on having a family gathering every four months that all the Diallos, no matter where they were in the world, had to attend. As next door neighbors and friends for nearly the entire twenty-four years they had shared the same Key Biscayne neighborhood, the Diallos had regularly invited the Wrights to participate in many of their gatherings, subconsciously melding the families over the years.

That melding had become even more deliberate

after Nichelle's mother died. At the time, Nichelle had thought Cin Diallo just felt sorry for them, but now, with the wisdom of adulthood, she realized that was what friends did for each other. Although she helped raise her two sisters after her mother had been killed in a car accident, because of the Diallos, she'd never been alone.

"I hear you and Wolfe are going off to Paris next week," Alice Diallo, one of the youngest at just a few weeks past her twentieth birthday, said with a sigh. "That's going to be so *romantic*." She drew out the last word with a sly smile.

"We're going there for work," Wolfe reminded her as he reached for a platter of ripe plantains. He forked some onto his plate and tilted his head to listen to what his father, seated to his immediate right, was saying.

"But Paris is Paris," Alice said. "When I went there after high school, I totally fell in love with the city and with this gorgeous boy I met there."

"You're always falling in love, Alice. I bet you don't even remember that boy's name."

"Names aren't important," Alice said dismissively. "It's about the feeling."

Good-natured laughter bubbled around the table. She was only twenty but had been in love more times than anyone else at the table. At least according to her. Every man she dated was susceptible to her declarations of love. Once, she'd even fallen in love with a woman. The family refused to talk about it, even though she kept bringing it up and wanting the family to recognize that she was now "queer." Just like all the others, that love affair had blown over after a few weeks.

"It's the city of romance." Alice pointed her fork at Nichelle. "You can't tell me you haven't thought about it."

Nichelle shook her head. "I've been to Paris before, remember? I spent a few days there while I was back-packing through Europe. It's a pretty city, but I didn't see any romance in it, just a lot of people using any excuse to make out in public."

"You're so cynical!" Alice made a dramatic motion with her fork, sending a piece of asparagus flying.

"Hey! Stop wasting food," Willa called out from the other end of the table where the flying vegetable landed.

"I'm practical," Nichelle said to Alice. "There's a difference. When I fell in love, it wasn't in Paris, but I think those feelings are just as legitimate, right?" she teased the young girl.

Wolfe caught her with a stare worthy of his namesake. "You've been in love?"

Nichelle winced, wanting to kick herself for saying anything about that failed affair. "Yes. Remember the Harvard professor I dated a few years ago?"

"That bourgie douche-bag?"

"Elia!"

Nearly the entire table exploded to scold the fifteen-year-old and youngest Diallo child.

"Don't act." She stared them all down. "You know none of you liked him. Especially not you, Wolfe."

Wolfe bit into a plantain, and Nichelle noticed that the fruit left a sheen of oil on his lower lip. He licked at it, but the glimmer remained, making his mouth look plump and bitable.

"He wasn't very interesting," Wolfe said in his driest tone.

"See?" Elia laughed. "And Wolfe usually likes everybody."

"You don't have to say everything you think, darling," her mother gently scolded.

Elia pouted and stabbed her fork into a piece of curry chicken on her plate. But she looked up at her big brother and grinned. Wolfe winked back at her, then smiled innocently at Nichelle when she took note of their exchange.

Mid-meal, the doorbell rang. Since they had dismissed the staff for the day, Glendon Diallo, Wolfe's father, got up to answer the door. He returned a few minutes later with Nala, Nichelle's best friend.

She grinned and hefted a bottle of wine above her head as if she'd just captured it in the wild. "Greetings, family!"

Nala looked as if she'd just stepped from the pages of a Goth magazine in a sheer black shirt flashing her sequined black bra, a black leather skirt and heavy knee-high boots, also black. She wore her hair long and straightened, the inky mass hanging over her shoulders and halfway down her back.

She made her way around the table to greet everyone with a kiss on the cheek, hug or handshake. When she made it to Nichelle's side, she dragged a seat up to squeeze between Nichelle and Madalie.

"Why didn't you just use your key?" Nichelle bumped Nala with her shoulder. Nala had been in the Diallos' lives as long as she'd been in Nichelle's, wholeheartedly welcomed into both families since she didn't have a family of her own. Her keys to both houses were symbols of that welcome.

"I didn't want to be rude," Nala said.

Glendon Diallo sucked his teeth. "How long have you known us?"

Nala laughed. "Good point."

Wolfe's mother slid a plate and utensils in front of her. "We're glad you could make it," she said, squeezing Nala's shoulder.

She thanked Hyacinth with a smile.

"I didn't think you'd be back from Brunei so soon," Nichelle said.

Nala grinned. "Hey, it's frcc food night. You think I'd miss that?"

Nala and Nichelle met when they were both twelve years old and modeling for the same Miami-based clothing line. It wasn't long before Nala found that she preferred being on the other side of the camera, and Nichelle realized she didn't like any part of the business.

Nala was an orphan, a trust-fund baby whose parents had been killed in a freak shooting in Miami when she was just a toddler. She was raised by lawyers entrusted with her twelve-billion-dollar fortune until she turned twenty-one. Despite all the things she'd been through and the financial fortune that could have turned her into an unbearable person, Nala was a wonderful friend, and Nichelle felt lucky to know her. They were as different as night and day—and just as necessary to each other's lives.

"So tell me, what did I miss?" Nala asked.

"She and Wolfe are running off to Paris together," Kingsley, the oldest, said dryly. Nichelle frowned his way, but he only arched a teasing eyebrow then winked.

Nala giggled and looked at Nichelle. "Finally, huh?"

The dinner was wonderfully long. They spent hours lingering at the table over conversation and laughter and trading stories. As the evening stretched toward midnight, the dining room emptied and people made their way to the large family room or to the terrace overlooking the pool to share cigars and more risqué conversation.

Nichelle snuggled into the hammock at the back of the house, nearly half a bottle of merlot swimming pleasantly through her system. Nala lay on the matching hammock a few feet away, snoring softly.

Light footsteps approached from inside the house. Nichelle turned from her smiling contemplation of her friend to see Wolfe standing in the doorway. The scent of cigar smoke clung to him.

"Hey."

He stood in the light, dress shirt unbuttoned to show the strong line of his throat, and draped perfectly over his wide chest and shoulders. He looked ready to head out on a date.

"You leaving?" she asked softly.

He looked surprised. "Why do you say that?"

She only laughed, saying nothing.

"Yes, I am." His mouth curved in a sinful grin. "A new friend called."

"The one who came by the office?"

"No, another one."

She shot him a disbelieving look, then shrugged. "Just make sure you wrap it up."

"Always." He didn't deny he was heading off on a booty call.

Nichelle shrugged off an unexpected twinge of unease. "Wait." She sat up in the swaying hammock. "Are your parents asleep yet?"

He frowned. "No."

"Then why are you leaving? I'm sure they want to sit

and talk with you some more." Although Wolfe loved his parents, he was often at work, or at play, seeing them maybe once a month tops, and sometimes not for very long. "You should stay," she murmured. "The new booty can wait until tomorrow at least."

She could see his eyebrow tip toward the ceiling, a considering look on his face. He was surprised by her request, she could tell.

"I'll see," he finally said, hands in his pockets.

Nichelle knew what that meant. "Okay." She lay back down. "Have fun tonight, wherever you end up."

He paused in the doorway again, shoulders broad against the light flooding from the sitting room behind him. "Good night."

"Don't let the strange girl bite," she sang out to him softly.

When he left, she heard Nala stirring nearby. Her friend sat up and swung a leg on either side of the hammock.

"Is he really going to leave his parents' house on family dinner night so he can go bang some random chick?" The disbelief was plain in Nala's voice.

"It seems so," Nichelle said. "He is a man, after all. I think it's biologically impossible for him to turn down booty." But even as she said the words, she winced. That wasn't quite true. Wolfe was actually a lot more discriminating than that.

As if reading her mind, Nala snorted with laughter. "If he caught every piece of ass that got thrown his way, he'd never get any damn work done. Hell, he'd never eat."

"At least not food, anyway." Nichelle smiled and

curled up in the hammock. It rocked from the movement of her body.

"Doesn't that piss you off?" Nala asked.

"What?"

"The fact that he's off screwing around when he could be here with you…and his parents?"

"No. Should it?"

Nala sighed. Even in the dark, Nichelle could practically see her rolling her eyes. The assumption that she and Wolfe were, or at least should be, together wasn't limited to people in the office. Nala and just about everyone Nichelle loved rarely missed an opportunity to tease her about him, insinuating that there was a lot more going on between them than she and Wolfe were letting on. But she'd never had any romantic or sexual feelings for him. Yes, he was the most interesting of his eight brothers. But that was all. There was nothing more to her admiration than that. He was gorgeous, but there were gorgeous men all over the place, especially in Miami.

"Go back to sleep, Nala."

Her friend cackled and flopped back down into the hammock. "And *you* should wake up, Nichelle. That man won't wait around forever."

Nichelle snorted, a bad habit she'd picked up from her best friend years ago. "The only one waiting around here is you. For a hookup that's never going to happen."

Only silence greeted her declaration. Apparently, Nala had taken her snarky advice and fallen back asleep. Annoyed, Nichelle stared up at the ceiling of the verandah, the hammock swaying with her weight, her mind drifting. To Wolfe.

Chapter 3

Paris was beautiful, just like Alice had said. The taxi from the airport dropped them off on a breezy and warm day bright with midsummer sunshine and the smell of baking bread from a nearby boulangerie. On the steps of the hotel, Nichelle drew in a deep lungful of scented air and basked in the skin-prickling heat of the sun. Wolfe had to nudge her up the marble steps and through the gold-trimmed doors, where the doorman watched her with an indulgent smile.

"This is nice," she said.

He laughed. "Yes, it is."

Despite her unexpected infatuation with the city, she was more than ready when it came time to unpack and meet Wolfe in his adjoining room for a prewar conference. His narrow windows opened out on to a busy street and a view of the Eiffel Tower. Sunlight poured in like a dream.

Still wearing her travel clothes, she sat across from Wolfe in one of a delicate-looking pair of chairs near the coffee table. Nearly every piece of furniture in the room was lined with gold and perched on spindly legs better suited to effete royalty than a pair of robust Americans. But Wolfe took everything in stride, making himself comfortable in the slight burgundy-and-gold chair that only emphasized his powerful masculinity.

"Let's go over this thing one more time," he said.

She wordlessly handed him the tablet with her proposal and the slight changes she'd made during the taxi ride from the airport. As they talked, Nichelle's gaze slid to the open window. Although she wouldn't admit it just yet, she'd love to go and play outside. Alice's glowing talk about the magic of Paris had affected her more than she realized. Even the sound of traffic flowing in through the fifth-story window, a soothing mix of cars, bicycle bells and voices speaking softly in French, was its own seduction.

She and Wolfe weren't slated to be in Paris long, and the client they were chasing was just as likely to tell them *no* as he was to say *yes*. And it was really just peanuts compared to the Quraishi account, the one she'd given Wolfe the proposal for in Miami.

Jamal al Din Quraishi was the Moroccan head of a multibillion-dollar research and development company that also dabbled in oil. Having him as a client would be a real coup. Nichelle had it from her sources that she wasn't the only one angling for his business. The competition would be high, and gunning for the Quraishi account was going to be a challenge. Luckily, she loved a challenge.

Nichelle stopped in midsentence when she heard her phone chiming from the other room. "One sec."

In her room, she grabbed her cell and frowned at what she read on the screen. "Favreau doesn't want to talk business until after three this afternoon," she said when she got back to his room. She paused to look at the clock. "Four hours from now."

Wolfe tossed his cell on the replica Louis XVI settee across from him with an impatient scowl. "But he did invite us to come to his restaurant for drinks and enjoy his hospitality." Apparently, he'd just gotten the same message.

"I'm not here to socialize with people I'd normally avoid at home." The bright sunlight teased Nichelle through the window, something beautiful and tempting she couldn't have just yet. "I came to close a deal."

Wolfe shrugged. "Well he's happily stringing us along. At this point I'm not even sure if he has any intentions of doing business with us."

"That little weasel better sit down and listen to reason. I am not in the mood." She threw another longing glance toward the open window with its gleam of sunlight.

Wolfe caught her eye and smiled. "You keep looking out that window like you have someplace to be. You want to test out the city of romance theory for yourself?"

Nichelle looked away, not able to hide her smile. It was sometimes disconcerting how transparent she was to him. "Not quite. But if Favreau is going to jerk us around for four hours, we might as well go do something interesting that involves sunshine."

The last time she had been in Paris was for a long trip

in college. She and three friends had only stayed in the city for four days before hopping on a train to Naples. The entire four days had been wet and cool, even though it was summer, the clouds and rain retreating for only a few hours at a time before enveloping the city once more in gloom. She'd been over Paris before they even left. But now, with the sunlight creating its particular enchantment, she could see glimmers of what everyone else talked about when they chattered on about Paris and its ambiance.

"Screw it," Nichelle muttered. "Let's just go out. Okay?"

Wolfe chuckled. "Okay. Just give me about fifteen minutes to change and make a quick phone call."

"Good." She headed to her room.

Like their offices, her hotel room was just like his. No surprises, although it seemed that she was already going to be spending more time in his room than in hers. They tended to take turns monopolizing one of the other's spaces. His room actually had the better view.

Nichelle exchanged her tights and loose blouse for jeans and a thin cotton blouse with a string tied at the throat. She tucked a few things into a small purse and was ready to leave the room within ten minutes when the open laptop caught her eye, a new message on her email screen. Then her cell phone chirped with a message. It was from Favreau.

My apologies. I have meetings for the rest of the afternoon but have the next two hours free. Are you ready to impress me? My offices in 30 minutes.

Damn. Nichelle's fingers tightened around the phone. But she took a breath. She knew the proposal for Favreau backward and forward but dammit, she had been excited about taking advantage of the Parisian sunshine. Phone in hand, she slipped through the door between her room and Wolfe's.

"Favreau just sent an em—" She almost swallowed her tongue.

Wolfe was naked. He stood in the middle of the room covered in nothing but the light pouring through the windows. A pair of briefs dangled from his hand, as if he was giving some thought to pulling them on, but he didn't move a muscle when she walked into the room. If anything, he stood even straighter to give her more to look at.

Oh my God... Nichelle's mouth went dry, and her eyes widened.

His body was angled slightly away from her, a hip and shoulder in her direction, intriguing shadows swimming over his skin. And he was breathtaking. Literally, she could not catch her breath, staring at what she'd never seen before. A man who was beautiful to look at, true. But, having him tucked firmly in the realm of family, she'd never have thought to wonder at what lay beneath his designer suits and expensive jeans. But now she knew.

After the first hot and consuming glance, she dropped her eyes.

His feet were big. The bones strong but delicate-looking at the same time. Narrow ankles, muscled calves. But instead of keeping her eyes low like she should have, she looked up.

Wolfe had solid knees with scars on them from his childhood spent climbing, and sometimes falling out of, trees. There was a mole on his muscled thigh, the blemish like a drop of cocoa on the thickly cut flesh.

She lingered over it, taking her time to visually devour the body she had missed for years.

His thighs were big enough for her to sink her fingers into. Spread wide, they allowed a clear view of his long and heavy sex. Nichelle swallowed and blinked as his body started to respond to her gaze, thickening even more before her eyes, rising toward the slats of muscle in his belly. She yanked her gaze up to his wide chest, pectoral muscles, tiny button nipples that she suddenly imagined flicking with her fingers then soothing the brief hurt with her tongue. His arms bulged with muscle. His shoulders were firm enough to easily take the weight of her legs, her thighs.

Nichelle gripped her phone and apologized stiffly past her throat that was dry as a desert. "Favreau wants us at his office in thirty minutes." Then she very carefully turned and walked back to her room.

Wolfe stood with his briefs clenched in his hand long after Nichelle went back to her side of the door. His whole body was a fist. Tight, hard and aching. He'd been frozen while she looked at him, aware of her cool gaze on his body that suddenly felt too hot. He had hardened helplessly under her intense scrutiny, the blood rushing inexorably south.

He called himself ten types of fool for allowing her to see his physical reaction to her. But that was what he got for not taking advantage of what had been offered to him a few days before they'd left for Paris.

Anise, a woman he'd met while on a business lunch in the Gables, had texted him with a classic booty call invitation. He'd wanted it. He'd wanted *her*. But when, at the family dinner, Nichelle looked at him with disapproval, as if it would have been the worst sin for him to leave his parents' house to sleep with some woman he'd only just met, he reigned himself in. He ended up spending the rest of the night and most of the next day with his parents.

Since then, he'd been too busy with work, getting ready for the Paris trip and working with Nichelle on the Quraishi proposal. He hadn't made time to seek sexual relief from anywhere else, and by the time he'd gotten on the plane for Paris, his body was more than aware that it was suffering through an unintentional dry spell.

He stumbled to the nearest open window and breathed deeply of the cooler air flooding over his bare skin. He had to get it together. They had a meeting in less than half an hour.

Somehow, he got dressed and met up with Nichelle in the hallway outside their shared rooms. Wearing her business clothes like a suit of armor, she acted as if nothing had happened. They made it to the meeting with Favreau on time and worked together to convince the idiot to spend his money with them, then they left for the hotel.

Strangely enough, it wasn't awkward. They talked business in the taxi on the way to the meeting and back. Then, at the hotel, they went their separate ways. There was no more talk of them exploring the city together. Nichelle went for a walk, and Wolfe left for the hotel bar and a double whiskey.

He'd been to Paris before, each time on business. It was just another city for him, with none of the magic that most of the women in his family thought it held. The Eiffel Tower was nice. The brie was pretty good. That was it. Still, he'd been looking forward to sharing the city with Nichelle and learning more about it. But his erection had perked up and ruined any chance of that.

At the bar, he quickly knocked back his first glass of whiskey. The second glass went down even easier than the first, and after the third he was feeling relaxed, easygoing. He reached for his phone and dialed a familiar number. It only rang twice before his best friend picked up. It was still morning, just after nine, in New York.

"Hey," Garrison greeted him. "I thought you were in France this week."

"You thought rightly, my friend." He kept his voice low, aware of the French dislike of audible public conversation. Even though it was barely three in the afternoon, the hotel bar was far from empty. "I'm calling you from a very French hotel right now."

"Everything going well there?"

Wolfe grunted. "Yeah. Well enough. We got the client we came here for at least."

"You don't sound that pleased about it." Faint noises came through the phone, a low voice from nearby.

"The guy is a prick but— Wait, am I interrupting something? If you and Reyna are still getting your honeymoon on—" Wolfe named his best friend's new wife, a woman he'd met a handful of times, the most recent being at their wedding where he was best man.

"Then I wouldn't have answered the phone," Garrison cut him off.

Wolfe smiled, swirling the whiskey in his glass. "I would've been disappointed in you if you had. The grapevine says wives don't take kindly to that sort of thing."

"For once, the grapevine might just be on to something." Garrison paused. "You doing good?" A hint of worry crept through the phone. "You seem a little agitated."

Was he agitated? Wolfe shifted in his chair and tilted his head back to stare at the ornate ceiling with the pale cherubs and half-naked goddesses, the European idea of public art. He swept his tongue across his front teeth, tasting the question he was about to ask. "When did you know you wanted Reyna?"

A huff came through the phone, Garrison's version of a laugh. His friend was restrained to a fault. When they were younger, and hell, he couldn't lie, he did it now, Wolfe often made a game of trying to make Garrison literally laugh out loud. A full guffaw was as rare for his friend as oilfields in Florida.

"What's going on with you? Did you meet a woman over there?"

"Stop deflecting. I'm serious. When did you know you wanted to take her to bed?"

Garrison breathed a sigh into the phone. "The day I met her."

"Really?"

"Of course. You feel the same way about nearly every woman you end up dating." If that's what he wanted to call it. The unsaid words made both men laugh. One more than the other, obviously.

Garrison's laughter trailed off. "If you haven't met anybody over there, what's going on? Did you accidentally drink the water?"

"I'm in France, not Nicaragua, Garrison." Wolfe avoided the more important question.

"You never know what those French people are up to. First it's snails, then before you know it, you'll be stuck in one of their miniature bathrooms with something explosive like Bonaparte's Revenge."

Wolfe almost choked on his whiskey. "Right."

A waiter, crisp in a white shirt, black slacks and a long apron, served the high table next to his. The table full of business people, most of them Canadian by the sound of it, clinked their glasses in a toast punctuated with a round of celebratory laughter once the waiter left.

"So what's got you thinking and drinking at three o'clock in the afternoon?"

Wolfe didn't bother denying he was at a bar. "Does a man need an excuse to enjoy his favorite whiskey?"

"Not every man needs an excuse, but you do."

He dropped his head back with a slow sigh. "I didn't used to be this predictable."

Background sounds came from Garrison's end of the call, the creak of leather, the tap of glass on wood as if he was having an appropriate drink of his own, probably coffee, at his desk. He didn't say anything, just waited for Wolfe to break the silence.

Wolfe stroked the whiskey glass with his thumb. "You know what I've always thought about Nichelle, right?"

"That she's too important to sleep with. Yes, I remember."

"Well, today I might have had a slight change of heart."

"She's not that important to you anymore?" That was Garrison's idea of funny.

"Keep it up, Kevin Hart." He gripped his nearly empty whiskey glass. "Today, things got a little messy."

"You slept with her?"

"You're just making all the wrong guesses right now."

"I know you want to sleep with her," Garrison said. "I'm simply making the logical leap here. So, if I know you, something happened that made her more appealing than usual, and you're fighting your typical pleasure-seeking impulses."

"Something like that. I want her, you know I do. But now she knows, too."

"What, she saw you staring at her shoes again?" Garrison knew that Wolfe had a thing for women in high heels. Especially *Nichelle* in high heels.

Years before, when Wolfe had the idea to bring Nichelle over to Kingston Consulting, he'd set up an appointment to meet with her. They communicated by phone and email for weeks before he saw her in person, all grown up, for the first time in nearly two years. She stepped into the restaurant where they'd agreed to meet for their business lunch, breath-stealing in black and white, an outfit that made her look like a fifties pinup model but that he later found out she thought of as business attire, some version of a uniform. The dress caught his eye first, but as his eyes went lower, he damned near swallowed his tongue. Her shoes, electric blue stilettos, fit her feet as if they were custom made, creating an elegant silhouette of the already beautiful contours of her feet.

His heart thudded loudly in time to her footsteps as she walked through the restaurant, attracting the stares of nearly everyone she passed. Nichelle looked as if she'd stepped straight out of his fantasies, deep burgundy lips, hourglass figure and shoes he immediately imagined her wearing in bed. *His* bed. He reined in his thoughts before they could go any further and had even managed, he hoped, to get through the meeting with his mind strictly on the business proposition he wanted to make her. Although it was hard, he kept his eyes firmly on her face for the entire two hours.

Yeah, Garrison knew all about that and had laughed at him, another one of his rare belly laughs, when Wolfe told him about the meeting a few days later.

"She definitely caught me looking," Wolfe said. "But this time, she was looking, too."

Garrison hummed a response that was all doubt. "Are you sure you weren't having another one of those dreams again?"

Wolfe dropped his head back against the seat and groaned. "Oh, come on…"

He finished up the call the same time he finished his whiskey, urging Garrison to go back to whatever he had been doing while he tried to do a better job of not lusting after his business partner.

But nighttime came and tore all his resolutions to shreds.

A dream brought him right back to that moment in the room: Nichelle in the doorway with the phone in her hand. Her slender but curvaceous body in jeans and a high-collared white blouse that would have been virginal except for the fact that it was completely see through. In real life, he remembered that she had worn a black bra beneath the blouse and that it was more than the wisp of material it was in the dream. But reality and dream blurred, then the dream became what he wanted.

In the dream, her eyes flickered over him, warming his body, pumping blood rapidly through him, filling him with hard intention. But instead of leaving, she closed the door between their rooms and came closer. Wolfe began to shake. He dropped the underwear from his hand and watched her walk to him. The sinuous dance of her body across the carpeted space between them; the twitch of her hips beneath the thick fabric of the jeans; her slightly parted lips as she stared at his body, then finally, finally at his face.

She may have said something, the dream Nichelle. Or it may have been Wolfe's desire to see those lips part, to hear her call his name. He turned and she touched his chest, tracing the line down the center of his body, down his belly that tightened hard from the light stroke of her fingers. Those fingers skated lower as she met his eyes and held them. His throat was too tight for him to swallow, his lungs incapable of holding or circulating enough air. She touched his intimate flesh.

"Nicki…"

He groaned her name while her hands clasped him, caressed the tip of him with her thumb. A flash of mischief crossed her face.

She sank to her knees in front of him. Her breath stroked him, then her mouth, then her tongue. Her fingernails dug painfully into his thighs, a counterpoint to the humid heaven of her mouth. She hummed her delight around him, and Wolfe exploded with pleasure. He woke up gasping, his belly wet with evidence of his release.

Nichelle was furious at herself. One look at Wolfe's naked body, and she had reacted just like every other empty-headed woman who'd ever seen him, damned near leaping across the room on top of him. Women literally came on to him every day. To get laid, all he had to do was point a finger or nod his head.

And because of this, Wolfe dismissed those women as if they were nothing. He shared a night or three of physical gratification with them, sure. But at the end of it all, they were forgettable, and he could and often did replace them every few weeks. Nichelle didn't want to be like that. Ever.

After the meeting with Favreau, she left to wander the city alone. Instead of going back to change into more suitable walking clothes, she attacked the city in her business blouse and skirt matched with her favorite sunshine-yellow heels.

The heels weren't the most comfortable to walk in, but they forced her to move slowly and take in all the city had to offer. She strolled through the Louvre's courtyard to the Pont des Arts, one of the bridges festooned with locks from people who thought they were in love. The wooden slats of the bridge felt precarious under her high heels, even more so when she looked down and saw the water of the Seine wavering beneath the dark wood.

She wondered if all those couples who'd put their locks on the bridge were still in love and still together. A few feet away, an Asian couple, the woman in a lacy wedding dress, the man in a white tuxedo, posed for a professional photographer. Did they think their love would endure if they took wedding photos framed in the locks of other people's love?

"I bet they won't last a year."

Nichelle nearly jumped out of her skin at the intimate voice near her ear. She turned. It was a Frenchman, or one who looked stereotypically French in close-fitting designer jeans, a T-shirt and a light scarf draped around his neck. His eyes were gray, and his mouth was framed by a sexy, well-trimmed beard.

"I won't take that bet," she said in response to his earlier comment. "They might end up lasting longer than we live."

"True," he said, but hardly looked repentant. "And maybe every fool who latched a lock to this bridge will end up dying happily next to the one they came here with."

"You're awfully cynical for someone who lives in the city of love."

"It's the City of Light, thankfully. The other name is just a dreadful rumor." He flashed her a smile and crowded close to her against the railing. She could smell his cologne, something musky, mixed with his body heat and clean sweat.

Nichelle knew what he was doing. He was handsome, and she was single. She didn't have a lover waiting for her at home and didn't need anyone's permission to enjoy someone of the opposite sex. But even though the strange Frenchman seemed nothing like Wolfe—he wasn't as handsome, and his smell was almost too sweet—Nichelle looked into the teasing flicker of his gray eyes and only thought of the man she'd left behind at the hotel. The man who had stood tall, wrapped in light and kissed by shadow, his virile nakedness stirring a hot ache in the center of her. Nichelle stepped back from the stranger. Her spine connected with the railing of the bridge.

"You're right," she said. "Who needs love?"

His pale eyes sparkled down at her. "Definitely not me." His gaze dropped to her mouth before connecting with her own. "Would you like to have a drink with me?"

She didn't even have to think about it. "I'm sorry, I can't."

He moved back a step, a gentleman. The sparkle in his eyes did not dim in the least. "You've broken my jaded heart today, mademoiselle."

"But I'm sure you'll be better by tomorrow at the latest," she said with a soft laugh.

The stranger brushed her arm with warm fingers. "I hope whoever you're pining for will adore you as much as you deserve." Then he took another step back, still smiling. He winked at her then nodded in parting, deliberately stepping between the photographer and his subjects on the bridge.

Only after he disappeared did his words register. Pining? Hardly. But without prompting, images of Wolfe from the afternoon came back to her in brilliant color. His body, readying itself for sex, the firm muscles under light. His face, frozen in concentration as he stared at her. No, she was definitely *not* pining.

Nichelle left the bridge and the crowds to dip onto a side street. Yes, the city was magical in the sun. What she had missed while in college seemed a bit of a tragedy now. If someone like that flirtatious stranger had tried to pick her up back then, she'd have much better memories of Paris.

Maybe you can make some better memories now. With Wolfe.

The thought froze her on the sidewalk, hissed sudden breath into her lungs. Someone bumped into her, a woman who begged Nichelle's pardon then kept walking and chatting on her cell phone. The sound of her own phone ringing shoved her back into motion. She answered without looking at the display.

"How is Paris treating you?"

She sighed at Nala's voice. "So far the business aspect is going very well."

Her friend immediately pounced on what she *wasn't* saying. "And the personal?"

Nichelle sucked the inside of her bottom lip. "I just saw Wolfe naked."

"Oh! I wasn't expecting that." Nala sounded positively delighted.

"Me, either."

Nala's impatient sigh fluttered through the phone. "So what the hell happened after the naked sighting?"

"Nothing happened. I walked out."

"But…?"

She drew a trembling breath. "He's hot, Nala!"

"Welcome to the world of eyes that see." Nala huffed in amusement and exasperation. "I can't believe you're just now realizing that."

"You know I don't…didn't see him like that." She didn't want to. She'd be damned if she would allow something as petty as sexual attraction to ruin the effortless business relationship she and Wolfe spent over three years building.

"Are you going to do anything about it?" Nala asked.

"No." Nichelle shook her head. "Definitely not."

"Hmm. Okay. Um…" A pregnant silence pressed between them. Nichelle could almost see Nala swelling with curiosity. Despite the gravity of the situation, she smiled.

"Okay. Out with it. I know you're dying to ask something."

A breath of relief came at her over the phone. "Oh, thank God!" Nala giggled. "Is he big? Cut? Interested in you?"

Nichelle strolled down the sidewalk, slipping past two women who walked side by side, smoking cigarettes and talking in rapid Spanish. A bicycle bell trilled from nearby as a biker warned a pedestrian who had wandered into the bike lane. She thought about not answering Nala's questions then decided it wasn't worth the inevitable aggravation.

"Yes. Yes. And I don't think so."

"What do you mean you don't think so? Did he or did he not get hard for you?"

"Well, he's a man. Of course he did, but that doesn't mean anything." Three boys in hip-hop gear boldly looked her over as they walked toward her. She held the phone against her ear, paying them little attention even as they leered in an obvious way, one of them saying something mildly obscene to his friends. Nichelle walked past them.

Nala chortled. "What happens in Paris, stays in Paris."

"Nothing is going to happen between us. You know how I feel about this business partnership."

But it wasn't just about business. She'd known Wolfe since they were children. From practically across the street, she'd watched him grow from an energetic kid to an awkward teenager and now into a gorgeous adult male. In all that time, she hadn't felt a flicker of attraction. Why now, after all these years? If she had a type, it was the over-educated man with an extensive vocabulary, articles published in obscure journals and a track record of romantic stability and fidelity. Not this worldly man who didn't take anything seriously other than his family and work, who had a different woman every other week and didn't seem inclined to settle down at all.

"I know." Nala made a soothing noise. "But don't beat yourself up over this, Nicki. Things happen. Feelings change. It's just another one of those things."

She sighed. "Okay." The dam had already broken. There was no going back. All she had to do was get her unexpected attraction to Wolfe down to a manageable level so she could still effectively do her job. "Thanks for talking me through it."

"What are best friends for?" Nala paused. "But if you change your mind and decide to get down and dirty with Wolfe, you have to tell me everything. Seriously."

"Goodbye, Nala."

She hung up on her friend's laughter.

Chapter 4

When Nichelle and Wolfe returned to Miami, she tried and eventually succeeded in pretending the charged afternoon in the Paris hotel never happened. And it seemed as if Wolfe had, too. He never mentioned it, never asked to talk about it.

On an early Monday morning, Nichelle sat behind her desk with Wolfe distractingly at the back of her mind. She scanned an email from Teague Simonson at Sterling Solutions. He wanted her to come in for a meeting and see if there was anything at Sterling that would "sate her appetite for bigger and better." She hit the delete button. The only thing she wanted from Sterling was for them to leave her alone.

Someone rapped on her door.

"Come in."

Her door opened and Wolfe walked in with Clint,

their general counsel. Wolfe closed the door behind him, his eyes resting easily on her, before heading to his usual seat in her office. Nichelle looked away from him after a single flickering glance.

Nichelle moved from behind her desk to lean against the front of it. She crossed her ankles and her arms. Wolfe sat on the small sofa and kicked his feet up on the small hassock. He sipped his hot chocolate Nichelle's secretary had left for him.

"Tell us the news, Clint," Nichelle said.

The attorney paused in the process of swiping a finger across the face of his tablet. "Nice shoes, Nichelle." He blinked down at her lavender Alexander McQueen pumps, a thoughtful look on his face, before going back to his tablet.

"Thank you, Clint." She smiled at him then glanced at Wolfe. He only sipped from the large mug and gave her a speaking glance, head slightly tilted, body relaxed yet predatory in the Tom Ford suit.

"Tell me something good." She looked at him but directed her words to Clint.

"I don't know about *good*," the lawyer said. "But I can give you some information you can work with."

"I'll take it," she said.

He nodded. "You know the Quraishi proposal is sound. You did an impeccable job, as always."

"But…?"

Clint grimaced, looking as if he'd had a bad attack of indigestion. "You might have to let this potential client go."

Nichelle abruptly straightened. She propped her hands on her hips and planted her feet wide. "Why?

This contract could bring in over five point three million dollars to the firm over the next two years alone."

"I know the numbers, Nichelle." Clint leveled a pleading look at Wolfe. "But I really think we might have to just give up on this one."

Wolfe tipped his head toward Nichelle. "Whatever she decides is what we'll do," he said to Clint.

Over the years, Wolfe had learned to leave the business of client acquisition to her. He was the money and brawn of their operation while she was the seer and fortune builder. It was because of her that the company was as successful as it was now. Everyone knew it. Although it sometimes took other men in the company a little while to know the power structure, and they usually turned to Wolfe for most decisions, she quickly showed them who held the reins.

Clint sighed. "Quraishi is a devout Muslim and family man. You already know that. He won't do business with Kingston because its partners—" he jerked a stubby finger at them "—the two of you, are not a married couple."

"Excuse me?" Nichelle didn't think she'd heard him right.

"Quraishi would think it's improper. You're a heterosexual couple working closely together in business, spending long hours building a company from the ground up. It's very intimate work. He's a traditional guy and won't simply accept that your relationship is platonic. You see how people here at Kingston act. They just think you've been incredibly discreet all these years."

Nichelle didn't give a damn what anybody thought about her and Wolfe's relationship. It was none of their business. She clenched her jaw. "How can we change Quraishi's mind?"

"Aside from getting married to each other, you can't."

"Isn't that a little extreme?" Wolfe's voice rumbled with annoyance, an echo of what Nichelle was feeling.

"This is not the eighteen hundreds!" she snapped. "That doesn't even make sense."

"I think it's stupid, but that's the way he runs his life and his company. There's no morality clause when you work for him, but I hear that if he ever discovers any infidelity or improper sexual dealings among his employees, they are immediately fired." Clint dropped his intense stare to tap out something on the tablet. "You can approach him with your proposal anyway. It's a really good one. But know that once he finds out the two of you are unmarried and working so closely together, you won't get past his secretary."

Nichelle crossed her arms, her nails digging into her elbows through the thin silk blouse. She had done her research on Quraishi and reached a similar conclusion. But she'd been hoping that another perspective would prove her wrong. She wanted the Quraishi account. Badly. It was the key to the future she and Wolfe had discussed when he first brought her to Kingston Consulting. She stalked across the room to sink into the couch at Wolfe's side.

"I want that account, Clint."

The lawyer shrugged and gave her a helpless look. "You could always *pretend* to be married."

"No," Wolfe said immediately, an indecipherable emotion flashing across his face too fast for her to see it. "That's unacceptable. As fun as it would be pretending to be Nichelle's man for a week, absolutely not." His jaw tightened, and a muscle ticked just under the skin. "I'm not going to jump through some ridiculous hoops just for a little money."

A hint of hot chocolate marred the firm curve of his lower lip. The wet smear caught Nichelle's eyes, making her want to stroke it away with her thumb. Or her tongue. She tore her glance away and pulled her mush brain back to the conversation.

"A *little* money?" Nichelle quirked a brow at Wolfe.

"Okay, a lot of money." He flashed her an annoyed look and a smile at once.

Their eyes met and held. A fluttering awareness took wing in Nichelle's belly.

She licked her lips. This was getting a little ridiculous. Damned near every time she looked at Wolfe now, she was ambushed by the feelings that had taken her over in the French hotel room. "Clint, could you give us a few minutes?"

"Take as long as you like. I have another meeting in about an hour." He left and took his tablet with him.

The door barely closed behind him before Nichelle turned to Wolfe. "I want this to happen."

"Easy, tiger." His smile was warm and teasing, but there was a hint of seriousness there. It was obvious he wanted her to really consider what she was going after.

"I have," she said, as if he'd spoken those words out loud.

Nichelle was competitive to a fault. She knew that and most days tried to channel it for good versus evil. This was for good. For both hers and his.

She leaned into him, a hand on his thigh. "Just say yes to this fake marriage, Wolfe. I can make Quraishi come to us. Kingston Consulting needs this. You know we do." She felt the big thigh muscle jump under her palm, and her thoughts derailed.

Damn.

Wolfe didn't speak. Early afternoon light tumbled through the wide windows to fall over his shaved head and the goatee framing the lush and slightly pink firmness of his mouth. In one breathless moment, Nichelle was pulled back to that hotel room in Paris. The Eiffel Tower peeking over his bare shoulder, the low hum of the air conditioner beneath the heavy thud of her pulse as she watched him and realized how easy it would be to cross the room and touch him. Then taste and allow herself to be tasted in turn. She pulled her hand from his thigh.

"Liars get caught," Wolfe said. If his voice was a little shaky, she chose to ignore it.

"We won't be lying," she said. Except for the lack of sex, they practically lived like a married couple anyway.

He gave her a look that forced a rueful laugh from her. She dipped her head to twine her fingers in her lap. "Okay, a little lie. But what's a little lie in business?"

"Are you sure you want to go there?"

She didn't hesitate. "Absolutely."

He pursed his lips, his lashes lowering in thought. "Okay. Then we'll do it. But we have to do it the right way."

What exactly was the right way to lie about being married?

"When do you want to go shopping for a ring?" he asked.

A ring? Her belly tightened oddly at the thought. She shook her head. "No. Let's not take it that far. Some modern couples don't even wear wedding rings."

Wolfe leaned close. The scent of hot chocolate from his lips and traces of his mint-and-mandarin soap overwhelmed her senses. "*My* wife will wear my ring." His voice rumbled with an unfamiliar intensity. He stood up and brushed invisible wrinkles from the front of his tailored slacks. "Tomorrow, we go find rings." He picked up his empty cup and took it with him to the door.

Now that the agreement was made to pretend, second thoughts nipped at Nichelle's conscience. Maybe this wasn't the right thing to do. She straightened on the couch. But if the alternative was to relinquish any opportunity of getting Quraishi's business, she'd rather risk the deception.

"By the way, your shoes are *very* nice today." Wolfe paused at the door, a smile playing on his lips. His gaze dipped to the lavender stilettos before climbing steadily, slowly, up her body. "I just didn't want my appreciation to get lost in the usual round of adoration from everyone else."

The expected "thank you," or even something dismissive, didn't find its way immediately to her lips. His gaze on her was like a hot touch. She shivered in her stilettos, aware that he was looking at her in a way he'd never done before Paris. She felt like a fumbling teenager, uncertain how to respond to the unexpected flirtation. It was flirtation, wasn't it? *Christ! Pull it together, Nichelle.*

"You could never get lost among the masses," she said finally.

Wolfe grinned. "Good to know, especially since I'm about to be the number one man in your life." With another body-skimming look, he left her alone.

What the hell had she just gotten herself into?

* * *

A few days later, Nichelle and Wolfe met at the pier near the Coconut Grove library. He'd had a meeting near Vizcaya and wanted to go home to change before meeting up with Nichelle. She took advantage of the location to have a solitary lunch at one of her favorite spots in Miami.

She stood at the railing looking out over Biscayne Bay and the flotilla of boats anchored in the glimmering blue water. It was strange being out of the office during the week and in the sun. She didn't like to think of herself as a workaholic, but there were far too many days when she was locked in the office from sunrise to sunset without taking advantage of the sunshine, which was one of the best things about living in Miami.

"I hope you're not contemplating jumping off this pier just to escape our fake marriage."

She didn't turn when Wolfe walked up behind her, his footsteps quiet against the wooden planks. She smelled him, fresh from the shower, a different aftershave today, something subtle with the hint of sage. It felt good to anticipate the sight of him, to wait until he was standing next to her, his arms draped over the railing, his scent pressed close to her, his shirt a light brush against her bare arm.

"*You* should be the one with jumping on your mind then." She turned to him finally. "I'm the one who talked you into this, remember?"

He had traded that morning's suit for a short-sleeved gray shirt worn untucked over dark jeans. Sexy. Edible. Other inappropriate words came to mind, but she pushed them firmly away. *Friend. Partner. Platonic.* Those were the words she should be focused on.

He leaned closer to press his arm firmly into hers, a teasing motion. "Once I'm committed to something, I'm all in."

For better or worse, so to speak, that was true. Wolfe was a man of his word who also backed up those words with action. Yet another reason she trusted and loved him. As a friend. Nichelle drank the last swallow of her sparkling water and put the empty bottle in a nearby recycling bin. "You ready?"

They walked the short distance to the jeweler Wolfe suggested. It was a store he'd used for years, apparently. He opened the door for her, a subtly marked storefront that was easy to miss if you walked too fast, and stepped in behind her. As they walked in, the bell above the door jangled. Wolfe was so close that his shirt brushed against her shoulder blades, and his breath stroked the back of her neck. She swallowed.

The store was small and narrow but brightly lit; every piece of jewelry on brilliant display. There was the usual round of diamonds, platinum necklaces, rings and watches. They had only taken a few steps inside when a door at the rear of the shop opened and a slender woman stepped through. She was dressed in a nondescript but obviously expensive skirt suit. Her hair, pulled back from her face in a tight bun, was glossy and woven with strands of gray. She wore little makeup and no jewelry.

"Mr. Diallo!" The woman welcomed Wolfe with a wide smile.

She looked very happy to see him. Nichelle frowned. Just how much did he spend in this place, and how much of a regular was he?

"Martine." He greeted the woman with a firm handshake and one of his warmest smiles. After introducing Nichelle, he turned back to her. "How is your father doing? I was sorry to hear about his heart attack."

The light dimmed slightly in Martine's face. "He's actually doing much better. The doctors expect a full recovery but insist that he stay at home and away from the store for a while."

"I bet he wasn't happy to hear that."

"You know Papa." Then Martine smiled and made a dismissive motion with her hands. Her business sense had kicked in. Enough with the small talk when there were people waiting to spend some money. "But it's good to see you and finally meet the woman you've decided to settle down with." She turned her attention to Nichelle. "You are absolutely gorgeous!"

"Thank you." Nichelle appreciated the woman's kindness. Even if it was motivated by the desire to sell Wolfe more trinkets.

"I picked out a few things after you called," Martine said. She waved them to a small antique table surrounded by four padded chairs. "Let me get them for you."

Nichelle and Wolfe made themselves comfortable at the table in time for Martine to return with four trays of rings. The trays were velvet-lined black rectangles that held some truly breathtaking pieces.

She presented one tray to Wolfe, a selection of simple gold and platinum wedding bands, and the rest, all filled with glittering diamond wedding sets, to Nichelle. Although she'd never been one to be impressed by jewelry, Nichelle had to admit the pieces were beautiful.

A radiant cut canary diamond surrounded by a square of smaller white diamonds immediately caught her eye. But it was too extravagant for a pretense. She didn't have to see the price tag to know that the ring, at least five carats, cost over fifty thousand dollars.

Nichelle pointed to a plain wedding set, a one carat diamond solitaire and a matching platinum band. "That should be fine."

But Wolfe had been watching her. "Try that on." He gestured unerringly to the canary diamond. "I think that would look better on you."

With the gleam of a potential sale in her eyes, Martine gathered up the yellow diamond and matching band. She was about to slip them onto Nichelle's finger when Wolfe reached for them.

"Allow me."

In his hand, the rings looked small. The pale fire of the diamonds flashed prisms of light in his palms. He reached for Nichelle's left hand before she could voice a protest. His skin was warm against hers, and firm. She couldn't stop the tremor in her hand.

"Ready?" His eyes held hers.

Was she? The pretense was her idea, but now, faced with a gorgeous ring and an intent man with his hand on hers, she felt another quiver of trepidation. But then reality set in. This was only going to be for a few days. She took a breath.

"Yes. Yes, I am."

He slid the rings onto her finger.

"A perfect fit." Martine smiled at Nichelle.

Nichelle looked down at her hand. The yellow diamond sat on her finger as if it was made for her. The stone was even more brilliant against her brown skin, the surrounding white diamonds haloing its impressive size.

"It's a pretty rock." She tried to sound unaffected, but even she heard the catch in her voice. The ring was stunning. It seemed criminal to use it only as a prop in a game of pretend.

"We'll take it." Wolfe slowly released her hand.

Nichelle cleared her throat. "Now it's your turn." She curled her hand with the ring on it, fighting the urge to put the fist in her lap. She glanced over the tray of masculine rings. It didn't take her long to find one that vaguely matched hers in style—a wide platinum band with a vein of small yellow diamonds running through its middle.

"Try that one."

It, too, fit perfectly. Nichelle gave Wolfe a teasing smile and echoed his words. "We'll take it."

At the counter, Nichelle insisted on paying for Wolfe's wedding band while he unflinchingly gave Martine his black card for her rings. Despite his insistence that she wear them out of the store, she tucked them in the scarlet box Martine provided and put them in her purse. Having the rings on her finger felt too real, too significant.

They walked out of the store and back out into the sunshine. Nichelle drew a trembling breath. "Let's go get a drink."

They walked the few blocks to Greenstreet Café and found a table outside. Although it was a weekday, it was close to lunchtime with plenty of people watching to be done. Nichelle leaned back in her chair and put her purse in the empty seat to her left, conscious of the seventy-thousand-dollar diamond wedding rings inside it.

When the waitress came to take their order, she immediately asked for a dirty martini. Wolfe got his usual whiskey sour.

"Tell me," he said once the waitress had gone. "What's wrong?"

"Did I say something's wrong?"

"Well, you're not wailing and gnashing your teeth, but don't pretend you haven't frozen up on me on the walk over here."

Nichelle pressed her lips together and drew a deep breath.

"Things have been a little off since France, don't you think?"

"Is this about what happened in Paris?"

They both spoke at the same time, their words tumbling over each other's. The foolishness of it made Nichelle laugh, and Wolfe's deep chuckle soon joined hers. Their mirth only tapered off when the waitress came back with their drinks. Nichelle took a quick sip and sighed at the sharp pleasure of the alcohol on her tongue.

"That was a little ridiculous, wasn't it?"

"Yeah, it's not like I haven't seen a naked man before."

She noticed Wolfe flinch. Then he shrugged. "As long as you don't compare me to some limp Ivy League professor with an inferiority complex, we're good."

Her mouth twisted into a half smile. "You were definitely not limp."

"Jesus…" But Wolfe laughed in a way that made them both a little more relieved and relaxed. "Did that make things awkward? Because that's not what I want."

"Don't worry about it." She didn't want either of them to focus too much on what happened. "I'm the one who walked in without knocking. Serves me right for getting an eyeful of Wolfe untamed."

"Why does that sound so weird when you say it?"

"Maybe because it makes you sound like some sort of rabid dog." She shrugged, still smiling. "I don't really know."

"Normally you know every damn thing." He sipped his drink. "But it's okay. Isn't it?"

"It is," she said. It had to be. "Things don't have to change between us because I know a little bit more about your measurements than I used to."

Wolfe laughed. "So are you impressed? Or should I invest in a gym membership? Or a penis pump?"

A crack of laughter shot from her mouth, but she refused to rise to the bait. "I think you know the answer to all those questions. I'm sure your women, and mirrors, give you plenty of positive feedback on a regular basis."

He chuckled, a pleased and masculine rumble. "So, we're okay then?"

"Yes, we are okay. About everything. Even the fake marriage and that damned diamond." She toyed with her martini glass but didn't lift it to her lips.

Wolfe hummed low in his throat. "So you admit the ring scared you a little."

"It's kind of impossible to ignore."

"I think *you're* already impossible to ignore." Wolfe lifted his glass to his lips with a teasing smile. "The ring is just another accessory to your radiance," he finished.

"Keep talking that way and you'll find yourself with a wife for real."

Wolfe laughed as if that was the funniest thing she'd said all day.

By the time the second round of drinks was almost

gone, they were both relaxed enough to act normally with each other. The ring in Nichelle's purse was just something she would think about at another time. Preferably when she didn't have the distraction of Wolfe near her.

Later that night, she called Nala. It was a long conversation, one of their marathon talks that lasted until nearly sunrise. She told her best friend everything, texted her a picture of the rings, told Nala how it felt, that tingling warmth when Wolfe slid the rings onto her finger, holding her gaze as if the moment meant something. But she didn't fool herself into thinking it was more than just another amusement for him. A fantasy of significance that any of the women who'd fallen into his bed had had before her.

Just before she hung up, Nala put on her serious voice.

"I'll be in Cannes around the time you're in Morocco," she said to Nichelle. "If anything happens, if you need anything, call me and I'll come."

Nichelle hoped she wouldn't have to make that call. But she hung on to the offer like a lifeline.

Chapter 5

In the hush of business class, as the lights in the plane dimmed to allow the passengers on the long flight an easy rest, Nichelle and Wolfe were wide awake and drinking red wine. They sat in adjoining middle seats, chatting quietly while the aircraft winged its way toward Marrakesh.

"I think we should consider investing in a company plane." Wolfe swirled the Chianti in his glass, his eyes half closed while he gazed at Nichelle, who lay fully reclined in her seat but curled toward him. Her wine glass was nearly empty.

"That wouldn't be cost-efficient for us. Pilots want too much money these days." Her words were only a breath above a whisper, giving Wolfe the perfect excuse to lean even closer. She smelled like sleep and Merlot.

"I'd fly the damn plane myself." He licked a drop of

wine from his lower lip, watching the slow rise and fall of her breath beneath the scarf draped over her throat and chest. "Three airports and twenty hours of travel time. That's ridiculous."

Nichelle wore what she called her "plane clothes," delicate-looking flats, leggings and a long blouse that draped down over her butt. A black sweater. All very respectable. Even modest. But he couldn't stop looking at her. At the way she managed to curl up in the seat toward him, the stretch of her thighs under the thin leggings more tempting than any nude stripper who'd given him a lap dance. It was a mystery. It was distracting. He needed to get it together before they landed in Marrakesh.

And he needed to get used to her in ways he never had before. She shifted again in the seat, and the thin sweater fell away from her thighs. He could easily imagine tugging up that fabric to get access to the plump curve of her butt, the perfect size for his hands. She'd moan as he lifted her up to straddle him, her arms falling onto his shoulders while her mouth lowered slowly to his. Wolfe adjusted himself in the seat. *Damn.*

She lifted her hand, her left hand this time, to adjust the scarf she'd draped across her throat for warmth. The diamond rings flashed even in the relative darkness. He caught his breath.

In a way *this* was worse, being distracted by the rings instead of thoughts of making love to her. In all his years of living, he'd never thought much of having a wife. But suddenly he had a woman sitting next to him with his rings on her finger. It wasn't just any woman, thank God, but there was something even more intense because it was Nichelle, *Nicki* to him since that afternoon in Paris. She knew him better than most people. This seemed more dangerous somehow.

She threw out an obscene dollar amount. "That's how much it would cost us to have our own private jet."

He looked at her, amazed. "How did you know that? Tell me you didn't just do that calculation in the past few seconds."

She smirked. "You're not the only one who's considered kicking frequent flyer miles to the curb. But even if the cost wasn't so damn high, I know you love this part of it, too." She made a vague gesture to the cabin full of people. The 747, the stewardesses ready with a drink or an extra pillow or whatever else he wanted, other whispered conversations around them. "You even love the airport. Freak."

Wolfe grunted. He pressed the button to recline his seat to the sleeping position. Sometimes it was scary how well Nichelle knew him. "Go the hell to sleep, woman."

Laughing, she threw a sleep mask at him, left handed, sending the big yellow diamond once again sparkling in the dark.

Nichelle's first impression of Morocco was *heat*. The metal stairs clanked under her ballet flats as she left the airplane with her purse over her shoulder. She was glad she'd taken off her sweater and stuffed it into her rolling suitcase before getting off the plane. At her side, Wolfe made a soft noise, of surprise and pleasure, when the heat hit him.

"I like this place already," he said with a low sigh.

It was the first time for both of them in Morocco.

They followed the path along the tarmac from the

plane to the small airport, passing under the signs in French then Arabic welcoming them to the Marrakech Menara Airport. Other signs in Arabic, French and English pointed them toward arrival and customs. Less than half an hour later, they left the long line with their passports stamped, their carry-on bags rolling along beside them.

"There's our ride." Wolfe nodded toward a man, tall and serious looking, with a sign that read Monsieur and Madame Diallo.

"And so it begins," Nichelle muttered. She felt more than ever the weight of the rings on her finger. Wolfe's ring seemed much more natural on him. She hadn't once seen him adjust his platinum band; he simply seemed to accept the fact that it was there.

Her better-than-average French wasn't at all useful in Miami, so she took particular pleasure in speaking it with the driver. Wolfe was content to lounge in the back of the Mercedes-Benz and let her do most of the talking. He spoke French, too, better than she did, but was busy taking in the sights.

Wolfe rolled the windows down, sighing in sensual appreciation of the hot desert air that poured into the car. He sprawled on the seat, legs spread wide, his left hand—with the all-important wedding band—draped over one muscular thigh. His profile was etched perfectly against the sharp blue of the Moroccan sky. He looked tired. *And sexy*, her traitorous mind supplied.

At the hotel, a vast and gorgeous white building in the Moorish style that Wolfe instantly said he admired, the driver took their bags from the trunk.

"Monsieur Quraishi will call you this evening after you've had a chance to rest," the driver said. "Your rooms in the hotel and any amenities you wish to enjoy have already been taken care of." He passed an envelope to Wolfe, then, with a crisp bow, got into his car and drove away.

Wolfe raised an eyebrow. "It almost feels like he's trying to get *our* business."

He tore open the envelope, his eyes moving quickly as he read the letter inside. He passed it to Nichelle. The letter, in formal and beautiful French, invited them to a party at Quraishi's compound later that evening. He would send a car for them; all they had to do was be dressed and ready promptly at six.

"Our host likes his pleasure before business," Wolfe said.

"That'll give us some time to check out the place." Nichelle tucked the letter in her purse and glanced at Wolfe, noting the tired slump to his shoulders. "And get some rest."

"Good afternoon, *monsieur. Madame.*" A dark-suited young man stepped from the automatic doors of the hotel. "Allow me to show you to the front desk." He took their two small suitcases and made his way briskly back into the hotel and the cool blast of air-conditioning.

"Oh, thank God!" Nichelle sighed when the artificial air poured over her face.

"Come on." Wolfe walked at her side, looking perfectly cool in his pale slacks and long-sleeved shirt rolled up at the elbows. "You've lived in Miami almost all your life. Why are you sweating this heat?"

She gave him a dirty look at the awful pun.

"Bonjour, Madame." Nichelle stepped past him to speak with the smartly dressed woman behind the desk. "We'd like to check in."

After she offered their names, a different uniformed young man took their bags and led them to an elevator and a room on the third floor. He opened the door for them, put their bags inside then quickly disappeared before Wolfe could even reach for his wallet for a tip. The air inside the room was deliciously cool. Nichelle sank into the long burgundy couch, barely noticing the decor. It wasn't stiflingly hot; that was all she cared about.

"This place is incredible," Wolfe said.

Unlike her, he ignored the comfort of the large couch to prowl around the opulent suite of rooms. Which, she could see from the comfort of the plush couch, was beautiful. The rooms were alive with color. The large cabinet, set up with alcohol of all sorts, was painted in lush shades of green and gold that made her want to get up and touch them. But she was a little too exhausted for that. Now that they were out of the heat, the long day of travel abruptly caught up with her. She closed her eyes and curled into the couch.

"You look comfortable." There was something in Wolfe's voice that she was too tired to catch.

She opened one eye to see him looming over her. "It suits my purposes." She closed her eye and snuggled into the cushions that smelled like amber, smoky and sweet.

"I hope so since there's only one bed."

Her eyes fluttered open. "Hmm?"

"You heard me." He flopped down beside her and gave her feet a gentle shove. "You can have it. Go. I'm too tired to act more chivalrous than this."

Wolfe kicked off his shoes and lay back to rest his head on the opposite end of the long and wide sofa, his feet stretching out to touch her hip. But Nichelle was too tired to care. She belatedly shoved him back, or at least the part of his foot she could reach, and curled up tighter on the long couch. Within seconds, she was asleep.

Nichelle woke to the sound of singing. A low, wailing voice. A man. She blinked and sat up, rubbing at her eyes. The sun was still high outside the windows, but its light was a soft gold compared to the brilliant white from when they had just arrived.

"It's the call to prayer," Wolfe said softly.

He lay on the opposite end of the couch, his body still where it touched hers.

The ululating voice drifted through the room, beautiful and heartrending, Arabic words she did not understand. Nichelle breathed quietly in appreciation, keeping still to allow the sounds to wash over her, into her.

When it ended, she opened her eyes to see Wolfe quietly watching her. He looked only a little wrinkled from his nap, the white linen shirt unbuttoned halfway down his chest, showing off beautiful and hard flesh, a glimpse of a flat brown nipple. Nichelle curled her nails into her palm, overcome by a nearly overwhelming desire to touch him. It would be so easy to crawl down to the other end of the couch and finish unbuttoning his shirt, peel the soft linen from his body, bite, kiss and lick every inch of bare flesh.

"It's beautiful, isn't it?" His gaze did not leave hers.

She could only nod, swallowing heavily as the sweet and thick need rolled through her veins. The places where their bodies touched, her hip and his foot through the two layers of cloth, shifted and rubbed. Nichelle pressed her thighs together and clamped down on the inside of her cheek. *Jesus. The next few days are going to be torture.*

"I've wanted to come to Marrakesh since I was a kid," Wolfe said softly.

"Why didn't you?" Nichelle pushed the arousal away, focusing on the conversation happening in the open instead of the one her body was having with his. She tucked her hip deeper into the couch, trying to put some space between their bodies. But the little relief she gained was quickly lost when Wolfe's sock-clad foot followed her skin, tucking into her with a slight and suggestive caress. *Was he doing this to her on purpose?*

But Wolfe was the picture of innocence when he shrugged. "At first, I didn't have time. I wanted to finish school. Then my parents said it was too dangerous. After that, work became more important to me than seeing the world." He sat up on the scrolled arm of the couch, his head resting on his upraised arm. "Getting Kingston Consulting up and running took up most of my time."

The arousal slowly faded away as he spoke. Or at least her awareness of it faded.

"I never thought I'd hear you say work became more important than enjoying life," she murmured.

They were caught in a delicate cocoon together, lulled into a gentle world made simply of their own voices, the lush beauty of the room, the faint smell of Moroccan amber that billowed up from the couch like fine smoke. It felt like blasphemy to speak above a whisper.

"Yeah. I used to call Garrison a workaholic." His best friend spent far too many nights alone in his office working on divorce cases that didn't change the world.

Or at least he had, until he met a woman who dragged him from his tower and into a fully lived life. "Sometimes I think I'm just as bad. I only hide it better."

"I disagree with that," Nichelle said. "You love chasing women too much to work that hard at anything else."

"Now that comment *I* disagree with," he said. "For your information, I haven't done any chasing since the day before the family dinner." His voice was low, rippling with annoyance, most likely at himself.

It took Nichelle a moment to realize what he was talking about. Then she understood what he'd just said. He hadn't been with a woman in over two months? "Are you serious? Why?"

"I haven't had the opportunity?" He made it a question, as if he didn't know why he hadn't slept with any of the, no doubt, many women who'd thrown themselves at him since that night.

"Maybe that means you'll have more focus this week." Not that he'd ever had any trouble giving his complete attention to work.

"Or maybe I'll just have a nice pair of blue balls, like a proper married man," he grumbled.

She chuckled, poking him with her toe. "You don't even know anything about being married."

"Yes, and I'd like to keep it that way. At least for a little while longer."

Then they were both quiet, bathing in the sweet silence of the room left behind by the late afternoon call to prayer. She only heard her own breathing, the faint scratch of his socked feet against the couch as he resettled himself, the whisper of traffic from the street below.

"I'm a little hungry," Wolfe said a little while later.

"Me, too." She'd been drifting back into sleep in the

cool and comfortable silence. She hadn't eaten much on the plane, instead drinking her way through a half bottle of wine plus several carafes of coffee (that still hadn't managed to keep her awake). "There's a restaurant downstairs," she murmured through her sleep. "Let's have some appetizers and proper drinks before we head out tonight."

Wolfe yawned and stretched, his long legs going rigid against her thigh. As he moved, his shirt rode up, exposing the flat plane of his belly, the sprinkling of hair disappearing into his pants. Nichelle licked her lips but, keeping her lashes lowered, did not look away. He was impossibly beautiful. And every time she noticed it, she was shocked she hadn't realized it before.

"Another brilliant idea." He grinned and scratched his flat belly. "I'm going to shower and wake myself up." Wolfe yawned again. "Unless you want to go first."

She shook her head. "You don't take long. I'll wait."

When he disappeared toward the bathroom, she sighed and leaned into the couch and into the warmth he'd abandoned. *This is not going well at all*, she thought. But that didn't stop her body from reveling in the male-scented heat he'd left behind. Her lashes flagged against her cheeks.

"We have about an hour and a half before the limo gets here."

She opened her eyes to Wolfe, fresh and gorgeous in smoke-gray slacks, a white dress shirt and paisley tie. He smelled of his favorite mint soap and a hint of aftershave. She blinked in time to see him grabbing up the matching suit jacket then walking away. His dress shoes, black and handmade Italian leather, tapped the mosaic tile floor. His backside was a firm curve under the gray cotton.

Nichelle bit her lip and closed her eyes again. *Dammit.*

She rolled off the couch and got to her feet. A shower. A cold one. And then she'd be ready.

Half an hour later, she was dressed in a softer version of her usual outfit—a black pencil dress with a high pyramid neckline—when she joined Wolfe in the living room. He shrugged on his suit jacket, tugged on the cuffs of his shirt. She noticed his gaze flicker down to her feet, an eyebrow rising at the scarlet, sky-high and curvy-heeled Walter Steiger pumps. A new purchase.

His mouth opened to say something, then he closed it. He took a breath and looked around him, patted his pockets.

"Ready?"

She grabbed her purse with her cell phone and the hotel key. "Absolutely."

After a quick and light dinner in the hotel restaurant, they agreed to briefly stop by the room to brush their teeth and otherwise freshen up before meeting the limo outside. When they arrived in the lobby, Wolfe put a hand on the edge of the elevator door to allow Nichelle out ahead of him. As she smiled her thanks, she caught the flash of a familiar face from the corner of her eye. She froze.

"What's wrong?" Wolfe released the door and came closer. He touched her arm.

"Isaac Franklin." She spat the name like the bad taste it was.

As if he heard her call his name, Isaac Franklin paused in midstep and glanced over his shoulder at her. The smile he had for the man he'd been walking with froze on his face. For a moment, it seemed as if he would keep going, but he straightened his spine and crossed the opulent lobby to approach her and Wolfe. *Maybe*, Nichelle thought and hoped, *he isn't here for the same reason we are.*

"Diallo. Nichelle. I'd like to say I'm surprised to see you here for the Quraishi account, but I'm not." His words killed her desperate hope before it could have any real life.

Wolfe nodded at the man. They barely knew each other, probably had only been to the same conferences and hotel lobbies where they were competing for the same accounts. Like now.

"It's a small world, and our business is even smaller," Wolfe said.

"True."

Isaac, the man who'd succeeded her at Sterling Solutions, the company she'd left for Wolfe, didn't like her. And he never bothered to hide that dislike, which was something she appreciated over the hypocrisy of his colleagues. It was more than just professional dislike, she knew, but she never let it bother her. She didn't care what he or anyone else at Sterling thought.

"We're late." Nichelle looped her arm through Wolfe's, too thrown to think about how touching him would make her feel. Her diamond caught briefly in the fabric of his jacket. "We'll see you soon, I'm sure."

Isaac nodded. "I'm sure you will."

When she and Wolfe stepped outside the hotel door and into the thick desert heat, the limousine and driver were already waiting. Black suit, white shirt, gleaming shoes. It was a different driver, younger and wearing a slightly flirtatious smile aimed at Nichelle. But he opened the door for them, shut them in the privacy of the dark limousine and rolled up the partition. The lyrics to a Beyoncé song flickered through her mind before she suppressed the images they inspired—her knees, the carpeted floor of the limo, Wolfe's gaping slacks, his mouth parted in a gasp as her own tasted the most intimate part of him—with a brutal bite of the inside of her cheek. The coppery taste of blood burst in her mouth.

"You okay?" Wolfe touched her hand.

"Yes. I'm good." She swallowed the metallic taste in her mouth but didn't bother with a smile. "Do you think we're wasting our time here?"

"Why, just because you know for sure that we have a little competition?"

She shook her head. Isaac was more than competition. He was the shark in their previously calm waters. She cursed softly.

"Relax," Wolfe murmured.

He glanced out the window as the car pulled out from the circular drive of the hotel and onto the main street. Mopeds, motorcycles, cars, horse-drawn carts all competed for the same bit of space on the pavement.

The sky was a bright and vicious blue. Clouds floated in the endless sapphire, barely there, as if they, too, were afraid of the sun's burning heat that gripped Marrakesh, a city that was such an unexpected mix of beauty, noise and spirituality.

"Don't tell me to relax." Nichelle twisted her lips at him, only half joking.

Normally, the sight of her old colleagues would only urge her to do better and be better, leaving no doubt that she would metaphorically drag them through that conference room by the hair and dominate them with a press of her high heels on their collective throats. But seeing Isaac had thrown her.

"Just relax," Wolfe said again. "Tonight is about checking out the competition. We didn't know before that we had any in town, but now we do." He turned from the window and glanced down her body in a slow and thorough gaze that he'd never directed at her before. "And you look very ready to stab the competition in the throat with those weapons you call shoes."

Nichelle hid her surprise. Why was this man reading her mind?

She crossed her legs, and the shoes in question lifted with the stretch of her leg, headed between the sprawl of his thighs. Wolfe only watched her with an amused smile, not trying to protect himself as she teasingly stretched out her deadly heel toward his crotch. He trusted her, the bastard. With a roll of her eyes, she dropped the threatening leg.

Wolfe laughed, then leaned forward briefly to tap her silk-covered knee. "You can kill me later."

He turned his attention back to the scene passing the window, a smile lingering around his mouth. He had no problem relaxing, his body swaying gently against the leather seats from the movement of the car. Nichelle couldn't help but notice that the pale material of his suit was the perfect foil for his cedar skin. Her fingers itched to touch him. She sat on them and tried harder not to stare.

Only when the driver opened the door nearly half an hour later at a mansion miles from the city center did she realize she hadn't thought about the "competition" once after Wolfe told her to relax. But he probably hadn't meant to distract her from her foolish thoughts quite *that* way.

The mansion was truly, truly opulent. All gorgeous curves and mosaics, straight out of the dreams of *One Hundred and One Arabian Nights*. It was a tall, three-story structure, more desert palace than everyday mansion, with ribbons of lights bordering the driveway. There were three other limousines farther up in the drive, empty and with the drivers standing nearby smoking cigarettes and speaking quietly to each other in Arabic.

"Bonsoir, madame. Monsieur."

Wolfe got out first and stepped back, offering his hand to help Nichelle out of the car. She shivered when his big hand closed around hers, strong and warm. Okay. This attraction of hers was stupid and had to stop. How many times had he held her hand? How many times had he helped her out of cars and she hadn't reacted this way? She suddenly hated Paris with a burning passion.

Nichelle thanked him for his chivalry anyway.

A uniformed man approached them. "This way."

Wolfe offered his arm to Nichelle, and she curved her own through it after a brief hesitation. She squared her shoulders, ready to face whatever the night would throw at them. They followed their escort through a long foyer toward soft conversation, the music of sitars and haunting Moroccan drums.

The party was in full swing. The man ushered them through high doors, into the thick of the party, a room scented with rose water, the sound of at least five languages rising and falling in conversation and weaving with the music that wasn't loud enough to be overwhelming. Their escort took them directly to a robed man holding court before an international group of business people.

He was short—shorter than Wolfe at any rate—and handsome with his sand-colored skin, closely clipped beard with flecks of gray, and flowing white robes.

"*Monsieur* Quraishi. Your guests."

The man, Monsieur Quraishi, excused himself from the circle of attentive men and women with a quick nod. "*Monsieur* and *Madame* Diallo. Welcome." His voice was a deep, booming bass, the perfect accompaniment to his gentle and paternal smile. "At last I can put a face to the memos and emails." As if he hadn't thoroughly researched them through every means available, social media included. "Your wife is even more beautiful in person." Quraishi's look was appreciative but respectful, his gaze lingering briefly on Nichelle's shoes. She sensed Wolfe's amusement.

"Even though I claim no responsibility for that fact," Wolfe said with a glance of admiration at Nichelle. "I am glad to reap the benefits."

If she didn't know any better, she swore he was flirting with her. He was either being a shameless opportunist or a very good actor.

"I've trained you well, Mr. Diallo," she teased him back.

Nichelle was very aware of the ring on her left hand, even though it was the right hand that Jamal al Din Quraishi lifted to kiss. He greeted Wolfe with a firm handshake and an appraising look that his genial smile could not mask.

"It's rare to meet a couple who work so well together," Quraishi said.

"The secret, if you call it that, is we keep our personal lives away from the office," Wolfe said, all smiling teeth and handsome sincerity. "Because of that, not many people even know we're married."

Nichelle forced herself not to frown his way. If that was the story they were going with, why did he even suggest they buy rings? As if Wolfe sensed her thoughts, he lightly touched her hand, a calming stroke of her ring finger. She did quiet her thoughts, but made a mental note to ask him about it later.

"Very smart." Quraishi squeezed Wolfe's shoulder with a conspiratorial wink. "Come, let me introduce you two to some of the competition and to some colleagues of mine."

Nichelle and Wolfe exchanged a look as they walked ahead of Quraishi. *Some* of the competition? It wasn't just Sterling Solutions they had to worry about?

It turned out that there were two other firms in the ring. Quraishi introduced Nichelle and Wolfe to the group of men he'd been talking with, including the head of a Canadian firm whose work they were already familiar with. Nichelle immediately dismissed them as any real competition, but shook hands with a respectful smile. It wasn't long before the other men and women wandered off with the excuse of finding drinks, leaving her and Wolfe with Quraishi.

"Thank you for your excellent hospitality," Wolfe said to him. "The accommodations are exceptional."

"Yes, you're already taking excellent care of us," Nichelle said with a smile. "We were pleasantly surprised."

"So the desert hospitality is not as harsh as you envisioned?" The sharp-toothed smile challenged her, but there was humor there, as well.

Nichelle amped up her smile and added a soft laugh for good measure. "We had no expectations, *monsieur*. But I haven't been so well cared for in years." She could feel herself floundering and willed her tongue not to stumble. "Your country is exceptional."

At her side, she could feel Wolfe's silent laughter. He was the politician of the partnership. Better at smoothing ruffled feathers and making people feel at ease. She almost sighed in relief when he came to her rescue.

"The hotel is quite luxurious, even by our standards," Wolfe said. "My wife is very pleased with our first visit to your country."

My wife. Nichelle shivered at the intimacy the words conveyed.

Quraishi reined in his smile, made it warmer and less challenging. "In that case, thank you. Your comfort is my pleasure. Anything you want here is yours." He made a wide gesture to the ballroom and the mansion around them.

"Yes, thank you." Nichelle glanced around again.

Just then, she saw Isaac and his companion from the hotel, a man she'd never seen before. They made a beeline for Quraishi.

Wolfe dipped his head, mouth brushing against Nichelle's ear. "I think that's our cue to mingle," he murmured low enough for only her to hear.

"Of course, darling." She nodded to their host. "Thank you again for your hospitality, *Monsieur* Quraishi. We look forward to talking with you more later on this evening."

Wolfe guided her to the bar, where they ordered

glasses of orange juice mixed with sparkling water. "So how do you want to handle this?" he asked once they had their drinks. They stood with their backs to the wall, appraising the room.

"Let's mingle," Nichelle said. "See what we can find out about the so-called competition."

"Sounds like a plan, General." He touched his glass briefly to hers, his firm mouth curved into an intimate smile at odds with his words. "Good hunting."

When they separated, at least a dozen pairs of feminine eyes followed Wolfe as he made his way toward one of the men they'd been introduced to earlier, the Frenchman. His strong and graceful stride, the swagger in his hips, drew an almost indecent amount of sexual attention, Nichelle's included. Before Paris, she'd never given any, or at least not much, thought to how women always flocked to him. But now the amount of interest he attracted made her grit her teeth. If they were really married, she wasn't sure she'd be able to handle it.

Nichelle took a breath and made her way into the fray.

After nearly an hour of mingling, Nichelle's attention began to stray. It took more to keep up the social face, but she smiled and asked questions, shared information, made small talk with the best of them.

"So your firm is based in Miami." A gorgeous man with lambent brown eyes and a subtle Arabic accent nodded in her direction. "It must be difficult to keep your attention focused on work when there is so much beauty to distract you." His eyes dipped over her body, more than implying she was part of that irresistible landscape he mentioned.

"Pardon me, ladies. Gentlemen." Wolfe appeared out

of the crowd to touch Nichelle's shoulder. He aimed a narrow-eyed stare at the man with her. "I'd like to claim Madame Nichelle for this dance." His jacket was unbuttoned, and a crooked smile shaped his mouth. She wanted to stroke the firm line of his lower lip in welcome.

He tugged her to his side. "Is that okay with you?"

She grinned at his mischievous smile. "Of course. You can sweep me away anytime."

He led her to the dance floor.

"Are you doing all right? You looked like it was time for a break. Especially from your new admirer." Wolfe growled in mock jealousy, and she rolled her eyes.

One hand pressed into the small of her back, and the other claimed her hand in a modified waltz to the sitar music.

"Not from him so much, but yeah." She blew out a breath, relieved that he knew her so well but also annoyed that she had allowed her exhaustion to show. Although she loved her work and the business of making people bow to her will, there were some days that she only had so much to give before she needed to replenish her internal reserves. And today, playing married, being tense in a room full of strangers and potential enemies, had her mind working overtime.

She was strategizing and planning, modifying her approach to the presentation she and Wolfe were slated to give the next day. She was nearly exhausted. But with Wolfe's arms around her, she felt the beginnings of a burst of energy. She tossed her head back to look at him.

"They had me on the ropes," she said.

"Never say that. Whatever happened to 'float like a butterfly and sting like a bee'?"

"This Ali is tired."

Wolfe drew her closer, turned her in the steps of the dance. "We're almost done."

But the tiredness was rapidly draining away. Electricity crackled at the contact points between their flesh. She was slightly breathless, but had the growing feeling she could go for hours. She slipped her arms around his neck and rested her head on his chest.

"I'm feeling better by the minute, husband."

His hands tightened briefly around her waist, and soft breath that felt like a quiet gasp huffed at her temple. A humming sound rumbled in his chest.

Despite her better judgment, she'd switched from orange juice to vodka tonics. Wolfe's presence and her irrational jealousy of the women following him around were leading her toward a tiny internal meltdown. Even with that, she couldn't deny the comfort and peace of his arms. That, at least, hadn't changed. The majority of the crowd—which was mostly Muslim, she assumed— wasn't drinking. Most of the Westerners made unending trips to the open bar, although she'd limited herself to two drinks over the past hour. In Wolfe's arms, she caught the slightly sweet scent on his breath. Whiskey. He had switched to alcohol, too.

The music pulsed, and she allowed it to take her away. She melted into Wolfe's strong arms. His legs brushed against hers, and butterfly wings of awareness fluttered in her stomach.

"Good," Wolfe murmured into her hair. "I can't do this without my better half."

If they'd both been completely sober, they probably wouldn't joke this freely about their "marriage." But in that moment, it felt like a harmless ruse, something to take comfort in rather than run away from.

"You're right about that," she replied.

Wolfe laughed, spun her into a twirl then drew her back into his arms. He was even more relaxed than usual. Seeing him like this made her realize just how tense he had been. It felt good. Too good.

"See any women here you want to take back to the room and introduce to your little friend?"

He gave her a teasing glance. "Little?"

She laughed. "Relative to the size of the rest of you then."

He chuckled, slipping both arms around her waist and maneuvering her into a more modern dance, hips moving to the sensual beat of the drums. She'd forgotten how well he could move.

"Anyway, I only have eyes for one woman tonight," he murmured.

Her heart thumped in her chest. "Liar."

"Never to you." The faint scent of his exertion brushed her nose. Sweat. His cologne. Whiskey on his breath. He jerked his head toward a voluptuous woman standing almost in the center of a group of nearly salivating men. "That's the woman over there. She's too beautiful to ignore, don't you think?"

She pinched the taut skin at the bottom of his jaw.

"Ouch!" He laughed and gathered her in his arms again. "I'm just joking. I'm being very careful who I pay attention to this evening." His voice was low and intimate, soft as he spoke into her throat in English. "I feel as if Quraishi is watching us."

"Of course he is." She couldn't stop the ache of disappointment that it was the job, his diligence about keeping up the appearances of their pretense, that made him pay this much attention to her.

Something must have leaked through her voice because he held her closer. "Not to mention you are the most beautiful woman in the room. Where else would I be but by your side?"

She shook her head, quietly laughing at herself and at him. "Dial it down a notch, Casanova. I don't think I'm that needy tonight." But wasn't she? Nichelle moved closer to him, wound her arms around his neck and linked her fingers. She briefly felt the contours of the wedding rings beneath her fingertips before her hands settled at the back of his neck. His skin was warm seduction. His breath touched her mouth.

They moved slowly against each other, her hips following his hips, rocking to the sensual music, a slow winding that poured the honey of desire steadily into her veins until she was overcome by sweetness. She wanted to kiss him.

"You keep looking at me like that, and I'm going to forget all about this pretense." His eyes flickered down to her mouth, and she licked her lips. He hungrily followed the motion with his gaze, and she drew a sharp breath at the jolt of heat in her belly.

Oh no, no, no.

She drew another sharp breath. "I think…" Nichelle licked her lips and tried again. "I think I'm going to get some fresh air." Then she carefully drew back from him, her aching and needy body, her arms, her fingers, her tangled thoughts. She turned and left. Nichelle fumbled her way through the crowd that seemed intent on keeping her in the small room and shoving her back toward Wolfe. But maybe all of that was in her mind. Maybe.

She found her way out to a balcony overlooking the courtyard. A mazelike garden made from fruit-heavy orange trees, purple and white bougainvillea, a large tiled fountain in its center. The night was scented and warm, its darkness heavy around her shoulders, broken only by the gentle illumination from the pair of floor lamps on each side of the wide balcony.

Nichelle drew deep breaths until her thoughts calmed. But her brain still fuzzed at the edges from the alcohol she'd had earlier. She wasn't a drinker, never had a high tolerance for alcohol. In fact, she only normally needed one drink. Drink number two was begging for trouble. And now, she found herself firmly in trouble. And in lust.

She twisted the rings on her finger.

"Are you well?"

The question, asked softly in French, made her jerk in surprise. She turned to face the source of the inquiry, although she could tell by the voice who it was.

"*Monsieur* Quraishi." She greeted him with a deliberately unconcerned smile. "Yes, I am doing fine. Thank you for asking." She curled her hands around the stone of the balcony, taking comfort in the firm and slick marble under her palms. "It's beautiful out here. I wanted to share it with my husband. He loves the architecture of the city."

Her host moved to her side with a whisper of his robes. He searched her face as if he was looking for something in particular, his deep-set eyes steady and astute. "Yes, Moorish design is some of the best in the world. There is nothing else like it on earth. It is beauty personified." His bearded mouth twitched, daring her to disagree.

But Nichelle wasn't anyone's yes-man. "Wolfe might agree with you on that."

"You do not?"

She weighed her answer carefully, hoping her intellect would override the alcohol that had nearly made her throw herself at Wolfe on the dance floor. "I do find it beautiful, yes. There is nothing else like it."

He chuckled. "Truthful while being diplomatic. I like that."

On the inside, Nichelle flinched. The guilt at their deception twisted unpleasantly in her chest. Maybe this hadn't been one of her best ideas.

Footsteps tapped toward them. "*Monsieur* Quraishi."

The man who'd escorted her and Wolfe into the party appeared around the corner. Isaac Franklin closely followed him.

"Yes?"

"A word, sir?"

Quraishi dipped his head toward Nichelle. "If you'd excuse me, *Madame*."

"Of course."

As he walked away, she noticed Isaac watching her with hawkish eyes. Suspicion and a barely leashed anger burned in his gaze. She kept her expression neutral and did not look away from him. Eventually, Quraishi's presence forced him to turn away.

When she was once again alone, she cursed beneath her breath. The balcony was hardly the sanctuary she'd thought it would be. But at least she'd stopped thinking about Wolfe, about stripping that mouthwatering suit from his body and climbing into his lap to suckle on his tongue as if she was starved for a taste of him.

Nichelle blew out a breath and straightened her spine.

This was a challenge, both her attraction for Wolfe and the unexpected complication of Isaac Franklin. She'd never backed away from a challenge in her life and wasn't about to start now.

Chapter 6

A hot knot of arousal burned in Wolfe's belly as he watched Nichelle walk away. For the more informal party, she'd worn something softer, a black dress that skimmed her curves, the neckline as high as most of her blouses and the hemline inches below her knees. But the silk emphasized the perfect hourglass of her figure, and each step in those very high red heels twitched the enticing curves of her bottom. He longed to watch her walk away just like that toward his bedroom. He licked his lips.

"Your wife is a lucky woman. My husband hasn't looked at me like that in years."

A woman stood near him—the one he had jokingly pointed out to Nichelle a few minutes before. She *was* beautiful. But not like Nichelle.

"Then he's a fool," he said about the woman's unappreciative husband.

She laughed. "Or maybe I am." She looked him over with a familiar, predatory gleam, taking in everything about him. Maybe she was the one finished with her husband and not the other way around.

"Can I get you another whiskey?" she asked.

She must have watched him closely enough to know what he was drinking. He'd cut himself off nearly half an hour before, but he suddenly felt the need for another drink. He wasn't getting what he wanted tonight, Nichelle in his bed, sighing his name as he licked and stroked her body to completion. Another drink was close enough.

"Of course," he said to the beautiful woman. "Lead the way."

At the bar, she asked the bartender for another whiskey on the rocks, light on the rocks. Without asking, the bartender gave the drink to Wolfe while the woman, Saleema, she told him, asked for orange juice, no ice. She thanked the bartender and slipped a two-hundred dirham note across the gleaming surface of the bar.

Saleema said something that Wolfe assumed was "thank you" in Arabic, then turned her attention back to him. They wandered through the crowded room, stopping occasionally to speak with other guests, before she led him to one of the low couches at the back of the room. Like Nichelle earlier, he was done socializing. But this, socializing at Quraishi's party, was business, and it didn't matter what he actually wanted.

In the middle of conversation about something forgettable, the man he'd seen earlier with Isaac Franklin invited himself to sit with them.

"Orlando Green," he said with a smile that was more of a snarl.

Wolfe shook his hand, resisting the urge to wipe his palm on his slacks afterward. Although the man was well put together—he'd worn a suit to the party like most of the businessmen there—there was something a little oily about him.

"So what brings you here, Diallo?"

"Probably the same thing that brought *you* here," Wolfe countered.

Green's face grew tight. But he forced a smile past a tightened jaw.

"There's no need to talk business tonight." Saleema put a hand on Wolfe's knee, then on Green's, bending over so the high collar of her dress dipped to show the tops of her breasts. Wolfe stiffened, although he noticed the other man loosening his jaw to give her a real smile.

"You're right, Saleema," Green said.

So they'd already been introduced. Interesting. Or not.

Wolfe took a sip of his drink for want of something to do. The whiskey burned, a hot kiss all the way down his chest. With the heat spreading through him, he leaned back in the couch and widened his thighs, incidentally shaking Saleema's hand from his knee.

He put on one of his charming smiles and asked her something he didn't really care to know the answer to. Saleema opened her mouth to answer just as Green looked past Wolfe to something that made his eyes widen in appreciation.

It was Nichelle.

She stood a few feet away, a hand on her hip, eyes locked on the knee Saleema had just been stroking. She lifted her eyes to his, then to the woman at his side. There was something dangerous in that look of hers, both a command and a threat. It wasn't an expression he'd seen on her face before.

Something low in him growled at it, recognized the look for what it was. When Nichelle turned and walked away from him, heading toward the exit, Wolfe did the only thing that made sense. He followed. He mumbled something to Saleema and Green, abandoned his too-strong whiskey on the nearby coffee table and walked quickly after Nichelle, keeping his eyes on the firm one-two switch of her backside. He didn't want to lose sight of her this time.

She took them down a wide hallway, a path that she seemed familiar with, although she'd never been to the mansion before. He didn't know where she was going, and he doubted that she knew, either. But her steps were certain, and he was only certain that he wanted her. He ached with the want, barely able to walk properly. They moved through a high corridor, past servants slipping silently in and out of rooms, down a wide staircase with a banister that was cool under his hand, the many tiles making up its design a small road map to wherever she led them.

He heard her high heels echoing from below. The smell of chlorine drifted up to meet him as he descended the stairs. An indoor pool. There were no windows, only the single set of stairs they'd come down together. Blue water rippled and reflected on the tiled ceiling etched with a blue-and-white starburst design.

Such beauty would make him weep if he wasn't already looking at the most beautiful woman he'd ever seen in his life. Distantly, he was aware he was waxing more poetic than usual. His mind wasn't quite all there, and feelings and impulses he would normally have under proper control were bursting all over the place.

There was no one else in the enclosed pool chamber except for them. No music. No distractions. Only the faint hum of the pool's filter, soft sounds of the water lapping against tiled walls. Wolfe followed the echoing rap of Nichelle's footsteps until she was only inches away.

"Why did you leave?" His voice came out with a growl.

She crossed her arms under her breasts. Combative. Confrontational. "You shouldn't have let that woman touch you."

"Do you think that's something you should concern yourself with?"

"Hell, yes!" Her shout echoed in the tiled room. "I'm supposed to be your wife, remember?"

"In name only, sweetheart." *Sweetheart?* When the hell did he ever talk to Nichelle like that? But the strong liquor was scorching a trail in him still, and he barely stopped himself from dragging Nichelle against his body so she could feel how he burned.

"Wolfe, you're acting like a whore."

His spine jerked tight at the insult. "Why? Because some woman I don't know wants to put her hands on me?"

"You're right." She turned away to pace the very edge of the pool. "You're just acting like *yourself.*"

He drew in a sharp breath, a gasp from the pain of hurt feelings. Was that how she saw him? "Nichelle, don't say anything else to me that you'll regret."

"Regret? Hardly."

She spun to look at him, tall and regal in the bright

light bouncing from the white walls. The wavering reflection of the water rippled on her face, her bare arms. Her mouth was red and moist in the undulating light, her curved body a wicked temptation. He flushed hot. He wanted to touch her. But beneath the desire, an unfamiliar emotion tore at him.

"I wasn't doing anything with her," he said.

He realized then that the emotion was regret. He felt like an idiot for allowing Saleema to touch him and for letting Nichelle see it.

"You didn't stop her," Nichelle said.

She turned and walked away from him again, heels stabbing the tiles. She didn't raise her voice, but she fairly vibrated with anger and frustration. "You could've jeopardized everything by flirting with her. What if anyone important had seen the way you were damn near begging that slut to put her hand in your pants?"

"That's not what was happening by any damn stretch of the imagination. Don't resort to unnecessary exaggeration."

She turned back to face him, raising an eyebrow in disbelief and anger. "Fu—"

He tugged her into his arms and kissed her. She stiffened against him. Wolfe swallowed her gasp of surprise. Their lips pressed together, a dry connection. A *forced* connection. Something that he had initiated against her will. Wolfe drew in a ragged breath and began to pull away, feeling awful, as if he'd crossed some line that could never be uncrossed. But she grabbed his arms and kept him close, melted into him. Her lips parted, and her tongue flickered out to stroke his mouth.

His mind spun out.

The slick heat of her tongue was his undoing. He

cupped the back of her head, angling for more of the sweet taste of her. His heart thudded hard in his chest with the realization that, *yes,* she wanted him, too. He pulled her closer, shifting his chest to rub the hardened peaks of her breasts he could feel through the layers of cloth. A shock of sound left her throat: need and surprise. Wolfe gripped her hips and pulled her tight against him.

He ached with a need he hadn't even known he was capable of feeling. His entire body was hard with it, muscles, bones and sex all at fierce attention to the things she was making him feel. Her fingers scraped the back of his head, nails raking the light stubble. Wolfe circled his hips into hers, telling her wordlessly of his need. Nichelle gasped again and drew back, stumbling away from him. Her eyes flickered down to the thickness in his pants, then away. Wolfe swallowed, pressed his lips together to stop himself from telling her what he wanted.

I want to make love to you. The words hovered just a breath away.

The need was rampant in him. Like that time in the hotel in Paris, he wasn't ashamed for her to know he wanted her. She was so damned beautiful. If he'd known there had been even the most remote chance of having her, they would have been screwing in his office, in that uncomfortable couch in her office she loved so much, everywhere she would let him. Wolfe groaned, shocked at the thoughts that spilled all too easily through his mind.

He opened his mouth to apologize.

"You don't mean it," she said.

The lipstick was only slightly smudged on her swollen mouth. Her breath came quickly, but her eyes sparkled with challenge. And she was more than a little drunk, just like he was. Wolfe shook his head.

"You don't know what I was going to say. You can't predict me like a company's stock prices."

But that wasn't true. She knew him. More than most, she knew him. Maybe she even knew the level of his desperate want. If she allowed him to, he would press her against the cool wall of their underground hideaway and sink to his knees in worship of her. He licked his lips at the thought of pleasing her that way.

"Nicki…"

"Don't! Don't call me that." She backed away from him again, controlling her breathing with visible effort. "You don't get to turn me into one of your whores tonight, Wolfe. That's not what this arrangement is about."

Her words were like a punch to the gut. "You could never be…that. Not to me or anyone." He cursed savagely and turned away.

"This is stupid," she hissed.

He breathed deeply, his hand on the banister. "It is. I think I need to sleep off whatever I was drinking and talk with you tomorrow."

He couldn't look at her without feeling the endless depth of his want. An abyss of aching feeling and reckless desire. It had come out of nowhere. One moment, he was prepared to endure the flicker of attraction he felt for her. And the next, his body flared to life, like a gasoline-soaked wick, and all he could think of was Nichelle, Nicki, her body ready to receive him, the two of them making love like sex-starved animals on the cool tiles.

Yes, he was drunk. But that was no excuse.

He looked at her over his shoulder. "Let's have breakfast tomorrow and talk, okay?"

She sighed, a steadying sound. "Okay."

He took a step toward the upper level. "I'll tell Quraishi that we're ready to go?" He framed it as a question.

"Yes." Her controlled breathing was audible in the cavernous room. "I'm ready."

Wolfe turned his back to her and quickly climbed the stairs as if the very hounds of hell were chasing him. But he couldn't outrun himself.

Chapter 7

Nichelle lay on top of the sheets staring at the ceiling. She could sense Wolfe's presence, as awake as she was, on the other side of the bedroom door. She felt a million kinds of foolish. How could she have allowed irrational jealousy to make her chastise Wolfe for doing what he'd always done?

But she remembered the flare, no the *explosion*, of anger in her chest when the woman put her hand on Wolfe's knee. And how he sat there and allowed it, as if she had an invitation to touch him in a way that Nichelle had never gotten to.

She turned over in the bed and groaned silently with embarrassment. This was not how she'd planned to spend the time in Morocco, burning with alternating waves of regret and lust for the man she hadn't even known she wanted until Paris. If she didn't know any better, she'd have sworn that he put something in her drink.

But she was never one to blame someone else for her own actions. She wanted him. It wasn't the best idea. She knew that. Getting sexually involved would only hurt them both, and possibly their partnership, in the long run. He treated women like tissues, and she didn't want to be the next one. But the ache for him had been so swift, so unexpected, that it took her by surprise and she could only stand, gasping, in the wake of it and hope not to wake up emotionally bruised and bloodied in the end.

Nichelle squeezed her eyes shut and rolled over, trying again for sleep.

She and Wolfe needed to talk about what was between them. But more importantly, they needed to convince Quraishi that Kingston was the best firm for the job.

Tomorrow was going to be a hell of a day.

The next morning, she woke up long before sunrise to the sound of rattling dishes and a door closing. She left the bedroom, belting a robe around her waist, to see Wolfe already awake in the sitting room of the suite, a room service tray for two and papers in front of him at the dining table.

"You're just in time," he said, voice rough with sleep. "Room service just left."

He was bare-chested, black pajama bottoms on, his face serious. She stared at his chest then looked away, flutters of arousal making her throat dry.

Would it kill him to put on a shirt? Nichelle lingered between the bedroom door and the table where Wolfe sat, acknowledgment of what happened between them last night on the tip of her tongue.

"Are we okay?" she asked.

Wolfe dipped his head. "Yes, we are." But his face was blank.

Nichelle ran her tongue along the inside of her lip, joining him for the small breakfast of mint tea, yogurt and Moroccan crepes. He poured tea for them both, the scented steam rising from the stream of sweetened mixture, his attention completely focused on the task. With a flicker of his lush lashes, his eyes met hers.

She gasped at the wealth of feeling she saw there— desire, frustration, resolve. He cleared his throat, and his expression went blank again.

"All right," she said. "Then let's get to work."

He nodded again and passed her the jar of honey.

Later, they were effortlessly in sync when Nichelle stood in front of the room full of mostly men and did her best to convince Jamal al Din Quraishi that Kingston Consulting was the best firm to help him create a successful long-term business strategy for his company.

She presented the raw data and the statistics while Wolfe backed her up by answering any questions related to logistics that Quraishi or any of his associates had. It was a perfect meeting, so perfect that Nichelle wondered just what she had been worried about before. Isaac Franklin was good, but while she had been at Sterling Solutions, he was never good enough to outperform her.

"That was brilliantly done." Yasmina, one of Quraishi's representatives, reached out to shake Nichelle's hand at the end of the meeting. "Thank you." She was sternly beautiful, her thick black hair pulled back from her strong-jawed face in a high, crowning bun. Her severely cut black skirt-suit hinted at a lush figure.

"It was our pleasure. Please don't hesitate to ask questions if there is anything we can clarify for you." Nichelle teasingly nodded her head in Wolfe's direction. "He can answer any queries that pop up."

"I already know the drill," Wolfe said. "I don't just stand around and look pretty."

Yasmina gave him a quick glance, an appreciative one, but she kept herself at a respectful distance. She gave Nichelle a subtle look, as if congratulating her on snagging such a fine specimen. Nichelle blinked, never having been the recipient of that kind of look before, congratulatory rather than avaricious.

"We'll be in touch with you within twenty-four hours about our decision," Yasmina said. "In the meantime, feel free to enjoy our hospitality for as long as you like."

Nichelle glanced at Wolfe.

"Thank you," he said. "You and Monsieur Quraishi have been very generous. We have a few things brewing in Miami so we'll be leaving soon."

Yasmina nodded. "Your wife tells me you are a fan of Moorish architecture, the desert and our way of life."

Nichelle knew Wolfe was looking at her. He probably wondered when she'd found time to talk to Yasmina alone and to talk about him in particular.

"Yes." He flashed one of his knee-weakening smiles. "I do enjoy your country."

Yasmina stared at him for a moment, seemingly stunned by his sheer beauty. Nichelle knew how she felt. Yasmina cleared her throat. "Please allow our guides to take you out into the desert and show you more of it. You will be bored sitting in an air-conditioned room for the rest of the day. Although I'm sure, if forced, you can find some ways of entertaining yourselves."

Though Yasmina's voice wasn't the least bit suggestive—she could have been talking about knitting and Parcheesi for all Nichelle knew—Nichelle blushed. It would be all too easy to fall into bed with Wolfe and spend the next few hours rolling around in the sheets with him and screaming his name until she was hoarse.

Nichelle nodded but did not meet Wolfe's eyes. "Thank you for that," she said. "We may take you up on the offer." Nichelle glanced at Wolfe, an inquiry in her gaze. "Yes?"

He nodded, almost looking bored. "Yes."

Yasmina nodded, everything decided.

"That went well." Wolfe stated the obvious when they were back in the limo and heading for the hotel. He shrugged out of his jacket and dropped his head back against the leather seat. "You were amazing in there." He winked at her before going back to his impression of a bored corporate tycoon. "But I don't want to talk about it until he gives us his answer."

"And Yasmina said they'll let us know by tomorrow." *It seemed like too much time to wait.*

"Yes." He'd also been surprised when the efficient woman promised them results sooner than anticipated. "So…the desert." Wolfe's eyes were closed, hands balanced on his thighs spread wide in the smoke-colored slacks. He was fighting a grin of excitement. Nichelle was fighting the urge to crawl into his lap and kiss the smile from his face, nibble on his bottom lip and lick the inside of his mouth until he made the same hungry noises from last night.

She shifted in her seat. "I think you'd like the desert."

And it would be a relief to escape the stifling intimacy of the hotel and the city. Maybe a desert ride was what they needed to put things in perspective.

He made a sound of agreement and reached for his phone to make the arrangements. Silk whispered against leather as she stretched out full length in the seat across from him and gladly allowed him to take charge of the excursion. She was drained from the performance but knew she wouldn't completely relax until they got word of Quraishi's decision. The next few hours were going to feel like forever.

Two hours later, after a meal and change of clothes, they strode down the front steps of the hotel again and back into the day's heat. Nichelle fumbled to a stop. Walking just ahead of them and dressed in casual clothes were Isaac Franklin and Orlando Green. Nichelle had a feeling that this wasn't just coincidence. What the hell was Quraishi playing at?

"I think we're going to have a little company." Wolfe's breath brushed her ear as he murmured the words.

She shivered from the contact and roughly corralled her attention before it could wander. "Unfortunately, I think you're right."

He straightened at her side, a hand tucked into the small of her back guiding her toward the Mercedes-Benz SUV idling at the curb. A driver, in the familiar black and white, stood holding the door open.

"*Monsieurs* and *madame*." The driver greeted them all with a formal bow, his hand still on the edge of the open door. He took Wolfe's bag and put it in the trunk.

Isaac looked at Nichelle with familiar and barely concealed dislike. "Ladies first," he said.

She shook her head with a cool smile. "Age before beauty." Then she tipped her gaze to Wolfe, giving herself time to get acclimated to this new situation. "That means you're last."

Wolfe gave a shout of laughter. "If I didn't know better, I'd swear you were trying to butter me up for something later."

"*Do* you know better?"

While the banter flowed light and easy between them, the two men got into the car ahead of them, having no choice but to climb into the two rear seats of the boxy but luxurious truck while Nichelle and Wolfe claimed the seats in the middle row behind the driver.

The truck smelled like new leather. If luxury had a smell, this was it—leather and wood mixed with the particular chemical tang of the air-conditioning. The truck pulled away from the curb with a throaty purr moments before mellow jazz began to play from the harman/kardon speakers.

In the seats behind her, Nichelle heard the shift of bodies against leather, and a low rumbling question she didn't catch. She sighed, not wanting to talk to either of the two men behind her. She scraped her nails through her short curls and leaned back in the seat. Beside her, Wolfe caught her eyes and smiled. In his gaze she saw the faint reminder of their night, the kiss, the restless evening they'd shared separately.

"Relax," he murmured.

He offered his hand, glancing down at her legs. She sighed, silently this time, not having the strength of will to stand up to the temptation he offered, even in the midst of their awkwardness. She did what he silently asked, what she always wanted from him, which was to slip off her red-and-black Jordan high-tops and her socks and drape her feet in his lap while she lay with her back pressed to the locked door. With the fine attention to detail that he did everything he thought important, he began to massage her feet.

His sinful hands stroked every inch of her feet, up to her ankles and her calves, while she breathed deeply and just barely stopped the most obscene noises from leaving her lips.

"Oh, God… I love you," she breathed deeply and closed her eyes. Wolfe's hands paused on her feet. His gaze touched her face; she felt it as surely as if he'd put his hand there. There was so much she wanted to say to him, maybe even *needed* to say. But she was very aware of the eavesdropping ears of the men behind them.

Outside the window of the SUV, the surroundings slowly changed from hotels and spas and nightclubs to languid stretches of desert as they left the clutter of the city behind.

The AC pumped cool air over Nichelle's face, nearly lulling her into sleep as she watched Wolfe with her feet in his lap. He looked so content that suddenly nothing mattered. Not the awkwardness that had been between them the night before. Not the kiss that sparked many dreams, and certainly not the bright diamonds that sparkled from her left hand.

She'd wanted to take off the rings once the meeting was over, but Wolfe waved a hand in dismissal of her discomfort. "The show doesn't end until we get back to Miami," he'd said.

She knew he was right, but that didn't make the rings any more comfortable to wear. Although, if she was being really honest, part of the discomfort lay in how *right* the wedding band felt on her finger. If she wasn't looking at it and obsessing about thoughts of a nude Wolfe, it would be completely natural to have it there, a beam of light between her and him, on her hand.

Over an hour later, the SUV pulled into the sandy drive of a house that seemed to appear out of nowhere in the flat, beige landscape. The house was white, a simple and squat rectangle with an attached verandah. In the yard, two hammocks hung parallel to each other under a large fig tree. One hammock was occupied while the other swayed, empty.

Just then, a man in gorgeous cobalt blue robes opened the door of the SUV and welcomed the four of them out into the desert heat. A dry wind blew against Nichelle's face and her bare throat. She adjusted the sunglasses over her eyes, glad she'd packed her darkest and most effective pair. The sun was a bright and oppressive presence in the sky.

The man in blue smiled widely at them. He was tall, and Nichelle had noticed that most of the men in Marrakesh were not. His height was a graceful counterpoint to his body moving like water beneath the calf-length robes. Incongruous acid-washed jeans and black flip-flops completed the rest of his outfit.

"Greetings!" he called out. "I am Mahmoud."

Another man, similarly dressed but in pale blue-and-white-striped robes, came up behind him. He bowed and introduced himself, first in French, then in Arabic, as Kareef.

"Mahmoud and I will be taking care of you this evening and through the night," Kareef said. "We will try not to lose you in the desert and earn Monsieur Quraishi's displeasure."

Although he was joking, there was something in the look his partner threw him, a warning and tight-lipped smile. But Kareef ignored Mahmoud.

"Come." Kareef gestured toward the house.

On the verandah, he gave Nichelle and Wolfe packs filled with bottles of water and face towels. Mahmoud wrapped a flowing piece of cloth around Nichelle's head and face while Wolfe watched, paying close enough attention that he was able to securely wrap his own when the time came.

The camels were already saddled and waiting in a patch of sand nearby, crouched on their stomachs, almost like cats, their backs burdened with large padded saddles and their heads and mouths harnessed with leading ropes. Even on their bellies, the beasts looked tall.

Nichelle narrowed her eyes at the camel closest to her. Its big eyes blinked back, placid as a cow's.

"Don't be afraid." Wolfe touched her back and she shivered, despite her earlier determination to shrug off his effect on her and act as if Paris had never happened. Or last night.

She looked at him as if he were crazy. But too late, she caught the glimmer of a tease in his eyes. He knew that he had essentially just challenged her to climb on top of this moving mountain and show no fear. She clenched her jaw. "Right."

"Madame." Mahmoud waved her toward the beast she had just been eyeballing. "Your chariot awaits." His French was fluid, flavored with something else that made it even more beautiful.

Kareef called out something to him in Arabic and he shouted back, not turning away from Nichelle. He guided her toward the camel. She held her breath, expecting a stench from the beast. But an accidental breath had her sighing in surprise. All she could smell was the dry desert air, faint sweat from the men and, very, very lightly, Wolfe's particular, masculine scent.

"Climb on and lean back. Relax and keep your thighs tight around her while she stands up." He nodded at the camel who almost looked…friendly.

Aware of Wolfe and his laughing gaze, she swung her leg over the large animal and held on to the front of the saddle.

"Hold on!" he called out to the camel, and the beast rose to her full height. Nichelle rocked in the high saddle, gripping it tightly from the expected but no less startling movement, the sensation of the ground receding even farther away.

Oh God!

The guide held the reins in his hand, watching to see if she was okay with the current state of affairs. When she nodded, he passed the reins to her.

"Hold these and wait."

Nichelle nodded again.

She controlled herself enough to see Wolfe taking a more graceful seat, swinging his leg in a movement that stretched his slacks taut against his backside. With a confident nod to their guide, his beautiful body rose into the air atop the camel as the animal stood up. Why did he have to be so damned gorgeous?

After seeing to Isaac and Green, the two guides mounted their camels with a minimum of fuss and led the foursome under the bright sun into the desert. Nichelle knew it was Wolfe's dream to be here in the heat with nothing around them, no cars, no city, no burdens. He had often shared with her while they sat in the aftermath of one project or another in the office, his tie loosened and her shoes kicked aside, that sometimes he just wanted to jump on a horse and ride. Keep going until the horse got tired and just see where they ended up. It wasn't about escape for him, but an exploration and love of the unfamiliar.

He sat atop the camel next to her, chatting amicably with their guides, his body swaying with the movement of the beast, as if this ride and this desert were the most familiar things in the world. Isaac and Green rode together at the very back.

"Yasmina tells me you are here on business," Mahmoud said to Nichelle, his brilliant blue robes blowing in the strong wind. "You are a woman of glass towers like her?" He seemed genuinely interested.

"Not like her." Then Nichelle shrugged. "Well, maybe. She is wonderful, whatever she is. I only met her a few days ago."

"Yes, she is wonderful." Something moved behind his eyes, more than admiration for the absent business-woman perhaps? Nichelle wondered how they knew each other.

When she asked, Mahmoud seemed happy to share. "My father worked with hers when I was a child. I saw her grow up."

Ah. Nichelle nodded. Mahmoud didn't seem much older than his midtwenties, handsome and relaxed under the desert sun, the turbaned blue cloth protecting his head, white teeth flashing as he spoke.

"I didn't realize she was so young."

"Yes. She has come very far from her station." He

looked proud. "One day, she will own that glass tower she works in."

Nichelle didn't doubt him. In just the few times she'd had the chance to speak with Yasmina, the woman seemed determined and strong-willed, allowing nothing, not even the perceived role of Muslim women, to get in the way of what she wanted. Her drive was inspiring. Nichelle said as much to Mahmoud.

"Yes, she has her eyes on the stars, that one."

But what about the diamonds scattered at her feet? It wasn't difficult to see that he was in love with her. Or at least something very much like love. He seemed to want the best for her. The longing in his voice was unmistakable.

"You love her?" she asked in English.

He was quiet for a moment, and she thought he didn't understand. Then he shook his head. "It is not my place to love one such as her," he replied in the same language. "I would only weigh her down and prevent her from reaching the glimmer above that she's always wanted."

Nichelle could identify with wanting everything. Sun, moon and stars. Even if she had a lover whom she wanted as much as he wanted her. But, if she had to choose, could she give up the glimmering heavens of corporate success for a chance at love? She didn't know. She'd never been in the position to choose. Her gaze flickered to Wolfe. As if he sensed her regard, he looked back over his shoulder. He hitched a brow, silently asking if anything was wrong. She gave him back a tiny shake of her head. *All clear.*

Mahmoud didn't miss a thing. He chuckled. "I see." They rode on, Mahmoud and Kareef telling them different facts about the desert, plant life, stories of Westerners getting lost under the burning sun and not found until their bones had bleached white in the hot sands. Wolfe laughed and encouraged them to tell more stories, the more gruesome and ridiculous the better, until Mahmoud and Kareef were trying to outdo each other with the most outrageous stories, the six of them laughing until the two-hour ride was finished for the afternoon. They stopped under a cluster of tall palm trees to drink water, tend to personal business and take a brief shelter from the sun.

Nichelle clambered down from her seated camel and found a big rock near the pond that rippled under the palm trees. An honest-to-God oasis. Sweat dripped down her back and between her breasts. Her thin jeans clung to her skin, damp in places. The turban she wore caught the sweat on her forehead, preventing the sting to her eyes. But she still squinted behind her sunglasses, actually enjoying the novelty of the experience. Who'd have thought it, this Miami girl surrounded by sand and no ocean in sight? She mopped her throat and chest with her handkerchief.

Wolfe looked cool and relaxed, laughing with the two guides. Yes, he was definitely enjoying himself. She looked up when she felt another presence. Isaac Franklin. His friend was sticking close to Mahmoud and Kareef, who had drifted, like most people, into Wolfe's irresistible orbit.

"So, who do you think will get this contract?" Isaac asked.

She immediately tensed at his fake good humor. They both had the mentality of sharks in bloody water, and she despised him for acting otherwise, especially out here where it didn't matter.

"That's not something I want to think about right now." She didn't bother to smile.

Isaac nodded as if she had just uttered the sagest of recommendations. Nichelle knew she had her bitch face on, but didn't feel inclined to change it. It was annoying enough that she and Wolfe had been herded together with Isaac and his colleague for this desert tour. She'd wanted it just to be her and Wolfe, for him to enjoy the journey without the annoyance of Isaac's presence to derail his good mood. Though to be fair, she was the one getting irritated. Wolfe seemed perfectly fine. A few feet away, he laughed with the guides, his head flung back, white teeth a brilliant contrast in his darkening face. She smiled from just the sound of his laughter.

Isaac didn't miss the direction of her gaze. "So you and Diallo, huh?"

"That's none of your business."

Yes, she was perpetrating a fraud for their would-be client. But she'd be damned if she'd discuss anything to do with her personal life with Isaac.

But he wouldn't drop it. "Everybody at Sterling thought that was why you left us in the first place. From what I hear around town, that's some first class pipe you left us for."

Nichelle drew a deep breath. No, she was not talking about Wolfe's sex game with anyone, least of all Isaac Franklin. She stood up and wiped off the bottom of her jeans.

"Go screw yourself." She turned and walked away.

The desert excursion was a challenge of some type. That was becoming more obvious with each passing moment she spent with Isaac. Quraishi hadn't just taken four people out in the desert on camels, all expenses paid, simply out of the kindness of his heart.

But Nichelle had to admit she was a little too frazzled to play whatever game was afoot. Her head wasn't quite there. She glanced again at the reason why and kept walking until she was just about on the water's edge, opposite where Isaac stood glaring at her. She wet her handkerchief and pressed it to her face, sighing at the relief from the heat.

After only a half hour at the oasis where they refreshed themselves, adjusted wilting turbans and drank water, their group prepared to move on.

Wolfe wandered over to Nichelle. "I wonder how much pee ends up in the water." He jerked his head toward the small pond where she had dipped her rag and wiped her face at least half a dozen times since they'd stopped. She noticed Orlando Green zipping himself up as he moved from behind a tree.

Nichelle glared at Wolfe. "I wish you'd kept that thought to yourself."

He chuckled and strolled over to his camel who rolled her big and moist eyes over to him as soon as he came within a few feet of her. Even the camel was head over heels in love with him. Wolfe playfully scratched her head and murmured soft nonsense in her ear that Nichelle was too far away to hear. Figured.

Then they were off again, riding beneath the desert sun with the sound of Mahmoud's melodic singing, Kareef clapping and providing accompanying laughter. The sunset, when they found it, was spectacular. They rode over the powdery sand, the edges of their turbans pulled down over their mouths and noses to block the sand being tossed around in the wind.

Nichelle's camel rocked beneath her while the sky turned to amber, then gold, catching fire above them as their small caravan rode toward a mysterious destination. She had done her job with the presentation. Wolfe was happy. They would go back to Miami soon enough. Even with the presence of Isaac and his sycophantic friend, the desert ride was an amazing experience she would not soon forget.

As the last of the light disappeared from the sky, they crested a mountain of sand. Nichelle exhaled in wonder. Below them sat a pair of large tents, white and stretched out beneath the darkening sky. A fire already burned a few dozen feet away from the tents, crackling and showering sparks into the air.

They had arrived at their home for the night.

Chapter 8

Wolfe sat around the fire with Nichelle, Franklin, Green and their guides, sipping from his small glass of mint tea. His thighs ached dimly from the ride, but overall he felt both energized and relaxed, completely at peace. His wants were few.

In the surprising coolness of the desert, the fire's warmth tempted him closer. But Nichelle's heat drew him even more. In her jeans and white blouse, she looked very much the modern woman, but with the winds howling through the sand and the camels only a few feet away, it was easy to imagine he was with her in another time and free of the responsibilities that had brought them to Morocco in the first place.

"It is a good night, yes?" Mahmoud nodded to everyone around the fire.

Wolfe nodded back. The trip hadn't gone quite as

expected, but he had enjoyed himself very much. Only one thing would make his desert adventure sweeter. He glanced at Nichelle. Her mouth was curved into a smile and her eyes sparkled with warmth. She looked happy.

"A good night calls for a good song," Kareef said. Then he launched into the opening words of Pharrell Williams's "*Happy*."

After exchanging a look and "why not?" shrugs, Wolfe and Nichelle started singing along. Franklin and Green looked at them as if they were crazy. The two men's uptight frowns only made Wolfe sing louder, while Nichelle's bright gaze warmed him like the midday sun.

The sing-along, scattered with talk of world politics, lasted until their Berber host brought dinner. They ate the small meal of chicken tagine over sweet couscous, talked and laughed around the fire until, one by one, the other men excused themselves for more restful evening pursuits. Franklin and Green went off to their beds in the tent while Mahmoud and Kareef wandered off to smoke, their deep voices in Arabic filling the night with another kind of music.

Wolfe sank lower onto his pallet in front of the fire until he was lying on his back and facing away from the tents. The makeshift bed inside the tent was more comfortable, but in the darkness of the desert, the stars were shimmering and bright. It seemed a shame to sleep indoors when this was happening in the heavens above him.

"Stay out here with me," he said to Nichelle.

He turned his head to watch her, similarly slumped in her pallet but much more gracefully, her long, jean-clad legs stretched toward the fire while a pillow she'd brought outside supported her neck.

She smiled at him, lazy and sweet. "Do you see me going anywhere?"

Once we get to Miami, yes.

But he said nothing. The profile of her face was awash in light from the fire, teasing out the fullness of her lips, her sharp cheekbones, the line of her neck. He couldn't think of any place he'd rather be, or anyone else he'd rather share the beauty of the desert with.

"I want to kiss you," he said.

She didn't move. He could've pretended she hadn't heard him. Except he noticed the flicker of her eyelashes, the shudder that rippled through her long body.

"Wolfe," she finally said, her voice softer than the breeze that fluttered the loose turban on his head. "This is the worst idea we've ever had."

He released a breath of relief, a breath he hadn't even realized he'd been holding. She wanted this, too. And she felt it, whatever "this" was. The pallet was soft under his back, the sand beneath even softer, and it moved when he shifted.

Nichelle stood up and grabbed the edge of her pallet. His stomach dropped in disappointment. She was going inside. But instead of heading toward the tent, she dragged her pallet closer to his until they touched. She lay down beside him, bringing her scent of honey and sage and sweat from their long day's ride.

"This is a bad idea." She touched his chest through his linen shirt and jacket, burning him. "Only here," she said. "This can't happen again when we get home."

He wanted to say *No. I want this all the time. We'd be so good together.* But the more desperate part of him simply wanted whatever she had to give him now. Anything that she would share. Her pallet, her breath, her lips. She hovered close to him, her breath puffing against his mouth, her hand making gentle circles over his chest.

"Wolfe…"

She kissed him.

A light touch on his mouth, a tentative press of warm flesh that made him gasp at the instant heat low in his belly. She hummed in approval and smiled against his lips. But he was beyond amusement. His flesh was on fire with a slow, pulsing need. That need built steadily between them as their mouths came together more firmly, no longer timid, both of them perfectly sober, perfectly clear-eyed and wanting. He settled a hand on her hip and carefully drew her close to him, allowed her to feel how much he wanted her.

He groaned. "You taste so good…"

Then he was done talking. Nichelle was soft and feminine and her mouth was a drugging, wet heat. Sweet mother of all that was good, he'd never felt anything like this in his entire life. With a touch of her tongue to his, he wanted to flip her over on her back and roughly take her and make her his. But he also wanted to treasure her, make sure that no one ever hurt her again, least of all him.

Her fingernails dug into his chest through his shirt, plucked apart the buttons to expose his bare skin. Arousal bucked harder in his belly. He licked the damp interior of her mouth, and she sucked on his tongue, a hot and suggestive suction that had him thick and firm in his pants.

He growled and pressed closer to her, then rolled

over until he was balanced carefully over her but cradled between her thighs. Her belly was soft under his hands, her nipples firm. Nichelle's breath hitched. She bit his lip, her hands drifting down to his sides, shoving up his shirt to get more of his overheated skin. He circled his hips into hers and they shivered together. His pulse was out of control, a mad riot under his skin. Wolfe panted into the soft curve of her neck, bit her. Nichelle whimpered his name. Her hand slipped under his shirt, an inciting warmth along his back, stroking the muscles hard and rippling from the control he was exerting over himself.

It would be easy to take this to its logical conclusion. To slip the jeans down her thighs, tug down his zipper, join with her in a way he had done before with countless women. But this was Nichelle. His Nicki. She was so many things to him that the act which should have been simple—muscle memory wrapped up with the unfamiliar emotions that made him grasp her body even more tightly to him—was not.

He wanted her. Wasn't it that straightforward? They were both adults. No one in Marrakesh really knew them. As far as these people were concerned, they were a married couple and didn't need anyone's permission to have sex under the stars. His thoughts skittered away with the slow stroke of her thumb over his nipple. He shuddered and jerked down into her.

"Nicki…"

Nichelle looked up at him, mouth open in a wet and hungry smile. "Yes, Wolfe?"

She lightly pinched his nipple, watching his reaction from under half-closed lids. Arousal drew Wolfe down to kiss her again. Her mouth was soft between his teeth.

She whimpered and the sound went straight down his middle, made him want to please her and show her he was there for her, no matter what she needed or how long she needed it.

He stroked her hip through the jeans, fingers hovering above her belt buckle. She arched up into him. Their tongues tangled and meshed, a slow and wet sound that dragged him deeper into the morass of lust and want. Her zipper slid down. Gasping, she wrenched her mouth from his when he touched her outside the delicate fabric of her panties. Wolfe stopped.

She whimpered again. "Keep going. Please."

That was all the permission he needed. Wolfe slid his hands into the underwear, parted her damp folds and found the source of her desire's heat. Nichelle breathed his name, a hot gust of breath against his neck. She fumbled against his bare skin, fingers clumsy in her lust, scraping and squeezing his nipples while she whimpered and twisted against him. Wolfe panted into her mouth.

She was hot and wet around his fingers, nails digging into his side while she rolled her hips, begging wordlessly for more of his touch. Her breath sped up. The motion of her hips on the pallet grew more desperate. Wolfe ached to fill her. But he ached even more to satisfy her.

"Oh my God. Oh G—!"

She sank her teeth into his neck to muffle her scream. He bucked with the sharpness of the pain but didn't stop touching her. She jerked her hips, and he encouraged her abandon with the curl and thrust of his fingers. Nichelle stiffened abruptly then shuddered against him, panting.

"You…" She licked her lips and tried again. "That

was so unfair." Her voice was broken as if she'd been screaming for hours.

Wolfe bent to kiss her again. But the noise of people coming closer pulled him from his stupor. He quickly searched the darkness to find Mahmoud and Kareef. They had finished their cigarettes and were coming back to the fire. Wolfe pulled his fingers from Nichelle's body, zipped her pants and pulled down her blouse.

Against him, she was lust-drunk, mouth swollen and soft. Her lashes fluttered down to hide her eyes, and she bit her lip. She looked vulnerable and delicate, the soft underside of her woman-in-charge attitude revealed. He didn't want anyone else to see her this way.

Wolfe grabbed a blanket from beneath his pallet and pulled it over her. She blinked in surprise. Then her eyes flickered toward the sound of the two approaching men. He dipped his mouth close to her ear, told her how much he wanted her and made a promise he intended to keep. Then he pulled away and put some necessary space between them. Nichelle rolled over onto her side, curling under the blanket and pulling it up to her ears.

The men came close, with a flurry of Arabic. But within moments they seemed to grasp the situation and vanish toward the tents.

"That was a little embarrassing," Nichelle said softly.

The light from the fire played over the planes of her face, revealing the subtle tremor to her mouth, its damp curve.

"Only a little." He made sure that the men hadn't seen anything. Just a married couple lying close together by the fire. She was fully covered up, and his aroused body pressed down into the pallet, away from unwanted eyes.

Wolfe touched her shoulder. "We should probably get some sleep," he whispered.

She nodded in the flickering light and rolled into him, bringing back her warmth and the salty intimacy of her scent. "This is just for tonight," Nichelle said. "It's cold and I don't want to go back to the tent."

Inside the tent was everything they'd come here to do. Business. Just like their pretend marriage was business—but Wolfe echoed her sentiment. For him, going back inside the tent meant a loss of their privacy. A privacy that the two Moroccan men had given them under the stars.

"Get some rest." This time she was the one who tried to soothe the situation. "I promise not to molest you while you sleep."

Wolfe smiled. "Don't make promises I don't want you to keep."

Chapter 9

The next morning, Nichelle woke to the insistent vibration of her hybrid satellite-mobile phone. Although they were ostensibly on a mini vacation, she kept her phone with her, ready to hear whatever Quraishi's decision was. She slid her arm under the blanket to reach for the phone, incidentally touching a warmth that did not belong to her. Wolfe.

She grabbed the phone, but her eyes tripped over the beauty of him stretched out on the pallet beside her, breathtaking in the rising sun. Her hand fluttered to her heart with the return of last night's memories. She tore her eyes away from Wolfe to answer and pay attention to the call.

"Nichelle Wright speaking."

"Madame." It was Yasmina. "A decision has been reached." Her voice gave no indication which of the

firms had been chosen. There was the general warmth, a pleasant camaraderie, but that was all.

Nichelle tamped down the feeling of impatience. "Yes?"

"We would like for you to come back to your hotel," Yasmina said. "I will meet you there at ten this morning."

"Very well." Nichelle peeled the rest of the blankets from her and ran her fingernails through her short hair. "See you then." She disconnected the call. "Wolfe."

"I'm awake." The words rumbled from him, low and sexy. His eyes stayed closed, though he moved his legs against hers, a smile on his lips. "What did they say?"

"We're meeting with them for a decision in a few hours. No hint about what it is."

He sighed and opened his eyes. "More games."

He shook his head, feet brushing hers again in a final stroke of intimacy as he turned away from her to stretch and yawn. She watched the arch of his neck, the muscles that rippled beneath his unbuttoned shirt. The memory of how the shirt came to be unbuttoned teased her: her hand against his chest, his thudding heartbeat under her palm, which echoed the frantic pulse between her legs.

He had felt so good last night, touching her in ways that made her whimper with surrender and need. If Mahmoud and Kareef hadn't returned, she wasn't sure she would've been able to stop herself from throwing away every ounce of decency just to have Wolfe under the stars. He had been the voice of reason, whispering his desire for her, but pulling away.

"I want you," she remembered him whispering. "But not here. I want to…" And he'd whispered filthy and raw things in her ear while he pulled away from her, inflaming her while depriving her of his aroused body and the means to sate it. "The next time I have you like this—" he'd briefly pressed his hardness between her thighs, curled into her, fingers tight on her hips "—I won't leave until we're both satisfied."

Nichelle trembled with the memory of those heated words. Much like she had trembled last night, wishing the two guides to hell for interrupting them but knowing deep down—very, *very* deep down—that the interruption was for the best.

It was one thing to lust after her business partner. It was quite another to actually make love with him and to share the physical satisfaction they both obviously craved. Even if it was the best sex of her life, once they broached that final intimacy, there would be no going back.

But what if the thing you can't undo is better than what you had?

She ignored the whiny voice in her head and drew back even more from the tempting man only a few inches away. She dusted the sand from her shoes and pulled them on, then started to gather up the pieces of her pallet. It took Wolfe a moment, but soon he was doing the same, getting himself ready for the trip back into Marrakesh.

Now that she wasn't completely absorbed in Wolfe and the promises of his hard and tempting body, Nichelle realized that the camp was already bustling with activity. A few yards away, a young boy was tending to the camels. The older man who had brought them dinner—and she assumed he was the one who'd set up the two large tents—stood nearby with his pale robes billowing in the breeze. He held a cell phone to his ear.

Mahmoud and Kareef came from their tent fully dressed and smiling.

"Good morning."

It was as if they had been waiting for Wolfe and Nichelle to wake before approaching the already ashen fire.

"Did you sleep well?" There was no hint of a smirk, no double meaning in his voice, for which Nichelle was extremely grateful.

"Yes, we did. Thank you." Wolfe answered for both of them.

"Don't worry about those pallets." Mahmoud handed them bottles of water. "A Jeep will be here for you in a few minutes to take you back to the hotel. It's faster than the camels."

"Why the rush?" Nichelle asked, although she assumed that getting back to their hotel via camel by ten was just not going to happen.

Mahmoud shrugged. "I do not know the minds of the rich. There is a meeting, they say. It is soon."

"Yes." Wolfe glanced at his watch. "Is there a place where we can wash up?"

"Inside the tents you will find everything you need, and an area behind it to tend to everything else."

Nichelle thanked Mahmoud and made her way toward the tent. When the car came for them, she felt gritty from the sand, but prepared. The night in the desert had loosened her up in ways she hadn't anticipated. She was still nervous about Quraishi's decision, but she didn't worry about it as much as she would have before. Instead, she was thinking about Wolfe. About being with him in *every* way. She ached with curiosity and with need. But she also knew that she'd have to leave both those things unsatisfied. For now.

She and Wolfe slid into the back of the SUV this time and allowed Isaac and Green to sit behind the driver. The SUV powered over the sand, roaring and rocking over ridges of high, powdery gold until they finally found solid road. Nine thirty caught them at the hotel, quickly separating from her former colleagues to head in for quick showers and more businesslike attire.

"You look beautiful," Wolfe said.

She paused in front of the full-length mirror in the sitting room of their suite, smoothing the black tie that matched the sleek faux masculine lines of her blouse and pencil skirt.

"Thank you."

Before, those words would have meant next to nothing. But now, after the night of shared kisses and sated desire, they held a universe of meaning. They meant, *I remember last night*. They meant, *I still want you*.

Nichelle tugged her gaze from Wolfe's. She shook herself and grabbed the hotel key and her small shoulder bag.

Wolfe stepped ahead of her to open the door.

The meeting was in a small conference room a few floors below them. The room was bare except for a long table and three manila folders in front of three chairs. No fruit. No coffee. They apparently didn't intend for it to be a long meeting.

Yasmina was already there when they walked in. She was talking with Mahmoud, who was dressed in a dark suit instead of the robes he had worn in the desert. Nichelle briefly met his eyes and smiled. He acknowledged her greeting, then quickly left the room. There was something going on here. She tilted an eyebrow in inquiry at Wolfe, but he gave only the smallest shrug. He didn't know what was going on, either. But the look on his face said he would soon find out.

Yasmina shook Nichelle's hand, then Wolfe's. "Good morning," she said. "I know you have other things to do so I will make this quick." Yasmina picked up a folder from the table and put it in Wolfe's hand. Before she could say anything else, the door to the conference room opened. Isaac and Orlando Green walked in. Yasmina excused herself to welcome them just as warmly as she had Nichelle and Wolfe. She gave them a manila folder of their own.

"Let me know if you have any questions," she said.

Wolfe handed the folder to Nichelle without opening it. "This is yours, whatever the answer."

She flipped the folder open with a casual hand, betraying none of the anxiety she felt. What she saw written inside made her draw a quick breath.

"Okay." Nichelle nodded once and gave the folder back to Wolfe. The brief flicker of a smile touched the corner of his mouth when he read the few lines written on the crisp sheet of white paper bearing Quraishi's letterhead and signature.

"Okay," Wolfe echoed.

Across the room, Isaac and Green were glaring at the contents of their folder, obviously not liking what they saw. Reps from the other firm in the running for the Quraishi account took their folder and glanced briefly at it before speaking with Yasmina then leaving.

"Thank you." Wolfe shook Yasmina's hand.

"I'll be in touch," she said, then lifted her head so the other men in the room could hear her. "Please have some breakfast in the restaurant downstairs with Monsieur Quraishi's compliments. If you need to follow up, please don't hesitate to contact me."

She smiled again at Nichelle and left the room.

Oh my God! Nichelle stood with her legs braced wide, hands crossed over her chest. They'd actually done it. Her knees shook, and her entire body went limp with relief.

"We did it," she said to Wolfe, barely whispering the words. They shared a look of satisfaction. Nichelle turned away from Wolfe's smile when footsteps sounded behind her.

"You don't play fair, Nichelle." Isaac stood far too close to her, his face a tight mask of anger.

"Fair?"

"You did *something*." A vein ticked in his forehead. "You cheated your way into this deal. I don't know how you did it, but I'm going to find out."

"No cheating happened, Isaac." She bared her teeth at him. "You always think there's some great conspiracy at work when it's just your own incompetence that cost you the prize. Grow up and get better." She tapped the folder against her thigh. "Now, if you'll excuse us, Wolfe and I have packing to do." No sooner had she turned away from Isaac and Green than Wolfe was guiding her toward the door and down the lushly carpeted hallway.

She felt like singing.

"Franklin seems to be taking this a little too personally." Wolfe's tone seemed deliberately casual. As if he was trying to ask her something that he didn't quite want to know the answer to. "Why is that?"

"He's a sore loser about everything." She shrugged.

Sudden tension radiated from Wolfe. His footsteps slowed. "Did you two used to be lovers?"

"No. But he wanted us to be." She started to say something about not ever mixing business with pleasure, but the memory of last night wouldn't let the hypocrisy past her lips.

"And here I was thinking he was just another stupid desk jockey." Wolfe looked relieved. "But he's smart enough to pursue you."

"I'm not sure if smart is the right word," she murmured wryly, remembering all the ridiculous things Isaac had done to get her attention while they worked together. Calling her father for permission to date her. Threatening to tattoo her name on his bicep. Asking her out on dates, multiple times, when she'd plainly told him she wasn't interested. He had been persistent. Then belligerent, when she firmly denied him in no uncertain terms. Somehow, he'd convinced himself she was just holding out for bigger corporate fish and would only sleep with someone higher up in the company than him. Isaac Franklin was the very definition of a sore loser.

Wolfe stopped walking. "Office hookups can be tricky." His eyes dipped to Nichelle's mouth then lower. He wasn't talking about Isaac at all.

"Yes, they can be." She licked her lips as her heart began to beat faster. There was a question in his eyes, a demand, and she longed to answer it. Nichelle stepped back until her butt hit the wall. Wolfe followed.

His breath brushed her cheek. "Why don't we—?"

"*Monsieur* and *Madame* Diallo!"

Wolfe broke off at their new client's voice. He stepped back, smoothing his tie. Monsieur Quraishi waited for them by the elevator, looking well-rested and dapper in a pale blue suit. "I wish I could have been there for the reveal, but my daughter had a concert nearby that just finished." He clapped Wolfe on the back and shook Nichelle's hand. "Do you have time for a celebratory lunch?"

"Of course," Wolfe said, although Nichelle wasn't hungry. At least not for food.

"We'd love to," she added for good measure, giving their new client a real smile even though, for one heart-stopping moment, she wanted to throw the account back in Quraishi's lap just so she could hear what Wolfe had to say.

Wolfe tugged down his cuffs and put his game face back on. "Let's go." His grimace could have passed for a smile under a certain light.

"Excellent." Quraishi waved them toward the entrance. "My driver is waiting outside."

He took them to a small restaurant near the Jamaa el Fna market. The chauffeur let them out near the depot for the horse-drawn carriages at the entrance to the square, and they braved the heat, winding through the madness of the square toward the restaurant.

"It is chaos here," Quraishi said. "But I would not trade it for anything."

A member of his security team, hardly unobtrusive in his dark suit and with the clear surveillance earpiece coiled against his neck, drifted behind them. Beggars emerged from the crowd to hold out their hands, to murmur pleas in Arabic and French. Wolfe, without hesitating, pulled loose bills from his pants pocket, passing out dirham notes to anyone who approached him. When one of the security team moved to push the beggars back, Quraishi waved him away.

He gently shook his head at a woman who came close, her head and face covered in a dirty hijab. "If you give to one," he said, "all fall forward with their hands held out."

As if to perfectly illustrate his point, another beggar materialized from the crowd, this time with a child on her hip. "*Monsieurs*," she murmured. "*Madame, s'il vous plaît.*"

Wolfe gave money to her, too.

By the time they had completed the short walk to the restaurant, over a dozen beggars had approached them, with more on the way.

"You are a kind man," Quraishi said. "I'm very pleased with my decision to employ your firm."

"But kindness doesn't equal effectiveness," Nichelle felt it her duty to say.

Their new client's eyes twinkled. "True. But it does make the working relationship, and the marriage, more pleasant."

At the restaurant, they sat upstairs on its terrace overlooking the square. The host seated them at a table under a wide, fluttering canopy, sun-washed white and reminiscent of the tent they had almost slept in while in the desert. Pedestal fans moved the air around them, keeping the terrace cool.

A sudden breeze floated up and brushed the back of Nichelle's neck. The same breeze flapped the tablecloth and caught the end of Wolfe's tie secured by a platinum tie clip. She gave in to the impulse to stroke the paisley silk. It slid cool and soft between her fingers and over his solid chest. They exchanged a smile. Nichelle turned away from Wolfe in time to catch a grin on Quraishi's usually reserved face.

"It is good that you two work and love so well together."

Nichelle's face heated, but she refused to act like some blushing, infatuated girl. "He is both easy to work with and to love." She deliberately did not look at Wolfe, but she sensed his amusement.

"She is neither of those things," Wolfe said. "But I enjoy a challenge." He grinned.

"Marriage should keep you on your toes, yes?" Quraishi said. "Complacency is the way to lose everything important in a relationship."

"We're not at that stage yet," Nichelle murmured. "My Wolfe is a constant source of surprises. Aren't you, darling?"

"Anything to keep you by my side," Wolfe said. His tongue, pink and damp, flicked out to touch the corner of his mouth.

Arousal flooded Nichelle in an instant. She swallowed and looked down at the napkin in her lap, fighting a blush. Quraishi chuckled with delight.

"By the way, before we go any further, please forgive my machinations regarding the desert trip, but I wanted to see how well you do under pressure. It helped me to finalize my decision."

The corner of Wolfe's mouth tilted up. *Is that what having Franklin and Green with them was about?*

Nichelle pressed her lips together. "As long as you got what you needed out of it," she said. "I know we did."

Quraishi chuckled. "I like your wife very much, Mr. Diallo. I think we'll all work very well together."

When the waiter came, Quraishi ordered nearly half the menu for their table, advising Nichelle and Wolfe what to try, telling them what were his favorites, and his wife's, as well. The terrace level of the restaurant filled up as they talked and ate, the noise of other diners rising around them while their own conversation dwelled on nothing in particular. Despite the pleasantness of the meal, Nichelle wondered why they were having lunch together at all. Why the celebration? Why the interest in her and Wolfe? Not that they weren't an amazing team. But still.

She noticed in her periphery when a group of Western women appeared on the terrace near them. The women were English and pretty, their familiar language oddly soothing after being enclosed within a French and Arabic speaking milieu for most of their trip.

Quraishi was explaining why she and Wolfe should travel to Essaouira, a nearby seaside town with a rich history and artisans who excelled in cabinet making, when a low voice in English interrupted them. It was one of the foreign women. This one was exceptionally pretty, with honey-colored skin and a tumble of curls down to the small of her back. A white dress made the most of her naturally dark skin.

"Pardon me for interrupting," she said to Wolfe. "But my friend over there—" she pointed to the table where four other women watched her with expectant smiles "—was wondering if you would be interested in going out with us tonight." A woman from her table waved at them.

The women were gorgeous and flirty, just the type that Wolfe would love in Miami. Nichelle knew he didn't take up every offer thrown his way, but when it came to carpe diem, he was a master. And the women, an international collection of beauties with their skin shades ranging from palest cream to oak, seemed like a temptation difficult for any heterosexual man to resist. Even if he was pretending to be married.

Quraishi looked amused as he sat back in his chair and watched Nichelle's face. He wasn't looking at Wolfe at all. Not even a glance. She schooled her expression into bland lines and turned her attention to her pretend husband.

Wolfe offered a smile to the woman, the smile that probably had her melting in her summer sandals. Nichelle had seen that smile, and the pleasant devastation it often left in its wake.

"That's very flattering," he said. "Thank you. But I'll be with my wife most of the day." He tilted his head toward Nichelle, but did not reach for her in what she was sure would have seemed like fake affection.

The Englishwoman clapped a hand to her mouth. "Oh, I'm so sorry!" she said to Nichelle. "I didn't know he was yours."

"No apologies necessary," Nichelle said in what she hoped was a gracious tone, even though inside she was seething. "This happens to us everywhere we go."

The woman stood back with a cocked hip, eyes flickering to Wolfe, although she was speaking with Nichelle. "It must be frustrating for you."

Is that what you're going with, bitch? "Not really." Nichelle stretched her lips at the woman. "He was gorgeous when I slipped the ring on his finger, and he's one of those lucky people who will be pretty until the grave. Women tend to notice that sort of thing." She dipped her head to the ring in question and smiled at Wolfe, who watched her with a careful expression.

The woman apologized again. "I'll tell my friends

he's off the market!" Then she left them to rejoin her own table.

Wolfe spread his napkin across his lap. "That went well."

Nichelle made a noise of irritation. "They didn't miss that damn ring on your finger. They all stared at you close enough to memorize the size of your inseam."

Quraishi choked on a laugh.

Nichelle abruptly realized what she'd just said, and in front of whom. "My apologies," she said.

"None necessary." Quraishi shook his head, still chuckling. "It was interesting seeing what a modern woman like you would do when challenged for her mate."

At the word *mate*, she looked at Wolfe again, who was noncommittally drinking from his glass of mint tea. *In for a penny, in for a pound.* Nichelle shrugged. "It really does happen all the time, though. Sometimes it's fine, because there is a certain amount of flattery involved. Women want this beautiful man I call my own." Their eyes met and Wolfe slowly lowered the glass, not breaking their gaze. "But sometimes, it can get a little irritating when rude women press the issue after it becomes obvious who I am."

As she spoke, she realized she was telling the truth. For years she'd watched women flirt openly with Wolfe, even slipping him their numbers when they thought she wasn't looking. It had all been blatantly disrespectful. She never blamed Wolfe for it. At least not always.

In the past, she *had* been upset when he returned the attentions of the rude ones who boldly came up to him when they were together. These women didn't care that he was a married or taken man. They were simply intent on getting what they wanted. If Nichelle saw two people dining privately together, she assumed they were a couple, even if their body language was distant. She would never proposition a man while another woman sat only a few feet away. With or without a wedding ring.

On the occasions she'd been bothered by those women and Wolfe's response to them, she lacked the emotional awareness to know *why* she had been irritated. But now she knew. She wanted him for herself. She might even...

Nichelle choked on a gasp. She swallowed. "You know, I'm actually not in the mood for lunch at all." She put her napkin on the table and stood. "If you'll excuse me, gentlemen."

Both men got to their feet, talking at once.

"We can leave now, *Madame* Diallo. It is no problem."

"Let me get a cab and we can go back," Wolfe said.

"No, please stay and enjoy your lunch." She pushed her chair aside to escape the sudden prison of the table. "I saw plenty of cabs near the square. I'm sure I can grab one to take me back to the hotel."

"Nichelle—"

"No." She stared at Wolfe. "Stay. I insist."

Then she fixed her face for her new client and offered her hand to shake. "I'll be in touch with you soon."

Then she was walking through the restaurant, past the women who all watched her with amused curiosity, and out into the sun. She drew a deep breath, cursing herself for allowing her emotions to push her out of the restaurant and make her look like a fool in front of Quraishi. But what was done was done. Nichelle straightened her spine and waded through the thick crowd in the square. It didn't take her long to find a cab back to the hotel.

Once in the cool confines of the suite, she called Nala. "I think I'm totally screwed here," she said in greeting when Nala answered the phone.

"Do you mean that literally?" Her friend sounded tired despite the teasing tone of her voice. "Because if so, this is not the time to call me. We can celebrate you and Wolfe finally sleeping together when I see you again."

Nichelle frowned. Their connection was incredibly clear. "Where are you?"

"A riad not far from the main square. When you told me you were having trouble keeping yourself together around Wolfe, I hopped on a plane. Cannes is only a three hour flight from here."

"Oh, thank you…" Nichelle sank into the bed with relief, glad for her best friend's impulsive nature and the love that she showered her with so completely. And of course, her ridiculous bank account that allowed her to jump on a plane from France with just a few hours' notice. She gave Nala the name of her hotel.

"Come pick me up. I feel like having the biggest drink in Africa right now."

Through the phone, she heard the hush of fabric on fabric, as if Nala was in bed and getting up. "Give me a half hour."

"Take your time." She instantly felt a twinge of guilt, knowing that Nala was more than likely still exhausted from her flight.

But an hour later, Nala texted to say she was downstairs and ready to buy all the drinks.

* * *

Wolfe watched Nichelle leave the restaurant, aware of Quraishi's thoughtful stare. He seated himself back at the table and rearranged the napkin carefully across his lap. Everything in him screamed to follow her and find out what was wrong. But the look she left him with as she said "stay" froze him in his seat.

Quraishi looked concerned. "Why are you letting her go?"

Good question. "She wants to be alone."

"Or does she want her husband to follow her and show her that these women, no matter how tempting—" He waved a hand toward the chattering Englishwomen. "—are nothing compared to her?"

"She knows that already." At least he hoped she did.

"But she may need to hear you say it."

Wolfe's hand hovered near his tie, twitchy with the urge to yank it off in frustration. They weren't married, dammit! And this situation was nothing new. Women came on to him all the time. Was she just putting on an act for Quraishi? Had she simply wanted to be alone instead of pretending through another endless public appearance?

"I'll give her the time she needs," he said.

Her face had been coolly stoic the entire time the Englishwoman talked to them. Nichelle didn't seem upset at all, simply bored. Even when she made the comment about certain "rude women." She'd simply been acting the jealous wife for Quraishi. Right? Wolfe picked up his now cold glass of mint tea and sipped.

"My wife is fine," he said finally.

But that didn't stop his mind from lingering on her during the meal. The business part of his brain was fully conscious of the things Quraishi outlined about their pending contract. But the other part of him remembered her face when the woman first approached their table. The flicker of annoyance that she had not bothered to hide. And he remembered the night they spent in the desert together. Waking up next to her. Her scent filling the waking morning and making him hard with need while an unfamiliar softness unfurled inside him, making him want to bring her closer to him on the pallet for nothing more than kisses and intimate whispers.

Quraishi tolerated his divided attention for another hour before asking for the check, his look both amused and understanding. When the car stopped in front of the hotel, Quraishi patted his shoulder. "Go to your wife. Show her there are no others. Tell her. Make her believe it since it's obvious you already do."

Wolfe thanked Quraishi for his hospitality once again and slipped from the car. On his way up to the room, he thought about what to say to Nichelle and how. But when he got to the suite, she wasn't there. He called her phone and, after it rang only once, got her voice mail. Worried, he sent a text. Seconds later, she replied with a brief message. She was out and would see him later.

Wolfe clamped down on his anger. What the hell was going on? Whatever it was, he couldn't stay in the room. He changed into his swim trunks and left for the pool. He exhausted his body with laps, his chest heaving, stomach and shoulder muscles aching with effort. But no matter how much he pushed himself, he couldn't stop thinking about her.

It was late when he went back to the room. She still wasn't there. So he packed his suitcase, getting ready for their flight back to Miami the next morning. He fell asleep waiting for her. One moment, he was sitting on the couch with his suitcase at his feet, and the next, he was opening his eyes at the sound of the door clicking open.

It was dark. Definitely past midnight. The smell of clove cigarettes came into the room with Nichelle, scents of a bar, something faintly alcoholic.

"Where have you been?" He choked out the question, not bothering to hide his anger and worry.

She froze in front of the door in surprise. The lamplight from the terrace highlighted her as she stood, looking slightly guilty. She wore the same clothes from earlier that day, but the collar of her high-necked blouse was unbuttoned. She carried her shoes in her hands. Then she seemed to shake herself and realize who he was, who *she* was. She visibly gathered her shield of coldness around her.

"In case your convenient memory has forgotten, I'm *not* actually your wife."

With a pointed glance in his direction, she slid past him for the bedroom then shut the door softly behind her. It wasn't until he heard the hiss of the shower that he realized she hadn't been wearing his rings.

Chapter 10

They went back to Miami and to business as usual. The firm settled into having Quraishi as a client. Nichelle and Wolfe stopped traveling as much. Days of sameness passed. If things between them weren't quite the same as before the Morocco trip, Wolfe blamed it on their differing schedules, on the additional work they had to do now that they were officially a million-dollar-earning firm.

He never stopped yearning for how things had been between them before, the ease they had had with each other, the feeling like it was the two of them against the world. But he also wanted something new.

Wolfe often woke from dreams of having her in his arms again, of filling her body with his love until they were both drunk with it, their voices rising in shared pleasure. But Nichelle seemed the same as ever. If it wasn't for the fact that he didn't see her as much as he used to, he could fool himself into thinking she was completely unmoved by what happened between them in Morocco.

As it was, she never lingered in the same room with him for long. She didn't put her feet in his lap anymore to demand a foot rub. She rarely came to his office.

As for Wolfe, he hadn't had a woman in weeks. Maybe that was his problem. He just needed to get laid. And because he was a problem solver, he immediately decided to do something about it, setting up a Friday evening date with a woman he'd met during a business lunch on Key Biscayne. Chantal.

Something about her had been interesting. It may have been that her cool, tall beauty, severe in a certain light, captivating in others, reminded him of Nichelle. How she seemed as cool as Greenland, but was a steamy and alluring woman of surprising lushness and warmth. Iceland, the woman. Or maybe he just wanted to make Chantal seem interesting. Either way, it was a date. And he needed the distraction.

A sharp and distinctive rap on his office door interrupted his thoughts.

"Come in, Philip."

His assistant came in with a vase of irises. "It's time for these to be replaced," Philip said, going immediately to the bookshelf where a handful of iris blossoms, just a little wilted around the edges, sat in an identical square vase. Wolfe started to tell Philip to cancel the fresh flowers, a standing order he had at the florist every week since he'd found out they were Nichelle's favorite.

With the sweet scent of the irises in his office, it was as if Nichelle was always there with him. A dangerous impulse, but one that he'd indulged in. The purple flowers lent an air of softness to the otherwise masculine space, he'd told her when she asked him why he kept the irises.

"Thanks, Philip." He let his assistant carry on without cancelling the flowers. Next week he'd do it.

"Of course, sir."

Philip took the old vase with him when he left. Wolfe immediately noticed the difference in the office, the hot and sugary smell of the fresh flowers that made him think even more about Nichelle.

He glowered at the vase, breaking his gaze only when his cell phone rang. It was his mother.

"Baby, am I interrupting anything?"

"Never, Mama."

His mother laughed softly through the phone. "I doubt you'd tell me if I was."

True. "I always have time for you."

"I'm glad you say that. How about lunch this afternoon?"

Just like he often called to check in on his mother, she checked in with him, too. It was something he didn't think she did with any of his siblings, even though he was sure he wasn't the only one who had figured out the family secret of her infidelity.

He mentally reviewed his calendar for the day. There was a project update meeting scheduled for one o'clock, but it wasn't anything he couldn't push back.

"Of course," he said. "Where do you have in mind?"

"I was thinking we could try out that new place with the fish."

"Oceana." He knew immediately which place she

was talking about. "The underwater restaurant that feels like you're eating in an aquarium?"

She chuckled. "Exactly."

As usual, she seemed to get a kick out of how alike they were. She and Wolfe had similar tastes in nearly everything—food, entertainment, wines. Even their temperament, a leaning toward pleasure simply for pleasure's sake, was eerily the same. It terrified him.

He opened his email and sent a quick note to the meeting participants to meet a half hour later. "Should I pick you up, or do you want to meet me there?"

"I'll meet you there, darling. I don't want to keep you away from work any longer than necessary."

"I'm the boss, remember? I can do what I like."

"Don't let Nichelle hear you say that," his mother teased. "I don't want her to blame me for your cavalier attitude toward your office responsibilities."

"Let me worry about Nichelle, Mama."

"As if you don't already?" she said with a laugh.

They met a few minutes past twelve. The elevator doors that took Wolfe twenty feet below sea level opened into a massive aquarium. The restaurant patrons were literally under glass and under the ocean, dining with sea life swimming languorously over and around them. A beautiful view. All the tables were situated along the transparent wall, leaving a long walkway leading back to the restrooms on one end and the elevator at the other.

The floor underneath his Italian loafers was hardwood and a deep brown, and the sound of his footsteps was absorbed by the low-grade noise of the already heavy lunch crowd.

His mother sat at a table near the middle of the restaurant. She had a glass of red wine, ignoring it in favor of looking around Oceana with a rapt expression.

"Mama." He leaned down to kiss her cheek.

"Darling." Her fingers lingered on his jaw before she withdrew it with a smile. "I hope you don't mind that I started without you." She indicated her wine. "It didn't take me as long as I thought to get seated."

"Good." Since Oceana had been written up in the *Miami Herald* and a few other places, he'd called ahead to ensure a reservation. It was very popular for a new spot that wasn't endorsed by a celebrity or porn star. "I wouldn't want you to wait for me," he said.

A waitress appeared at their table and handed him two sleek menus. "Welcome to Oceana, sir. Madam. May I get you something to drink?"

He ordered sparkling water, glanced quickly at the menu and ordered the fish of the day. His mother asked for the same.

"So what's happening in your life these days, my Wolfe? I never can get a moment alone with you when you come home for family dinner."

"That's the struggle of having thirteen children and not as many pairs of ears." He smiled, leaning back in his chair.

She looked beautiful. Two years away from sixty, but with a deep and dewy mahogany skin that made her look no older than forty. She wore her long, silver hair in a loose bun. Subtle makeup highlighted her mischievous eyes and mobile mouth, the soft curve of her chin.

She wore an indigo dress and black low-heeled shoes,

with touches of gold jewelry at her wrists and throat. Her wedding rings winked in the soft, undersea light.

"No struggle, love. Only a pleasure." The words she spoke were the truth, Wolfe knew, but she hadn't always felt that way. Hence the reason she had left her family for another man.

"I'm glad, Mama."

They had never talked openly about her betrayal, only circled the obvious empty space of words between them, what had happened the morning Wolfe, at twenty years old, had come to her with the small wooden box he found in her office after a long and thorough search. The box held a lipstick-stained silk tie, a small book of Neruda's love poetry and a photograph of her seated in a man's lap and looking defiantly happy.

His mother's face had caved in on itself when he gave her the box, the happy spark in her eyes abruptly extinguished. Later that night, he woke to the smell of smoke and looked downstairs from his bedroom window to see her burning the contents of the box in a copper bowl. She held the empty box in her hand, staring off into space while tears tracked down her cheeks.

"Here you are, sir." The waitress reappeared carrying an empty glass with a slice of lime perched on its edge, along with a bottle of Perrier. "Can I get you anything else while your meal is being prepared?"

Wolfe's mother met his gaze, a brow raised, a tiny smile at the corner of her mouth. "Yes, darling. Are you content? Or would you like something else?"

"I'm good for now." He nodded at the waitress. "Thank you."

She disappeared from the table, leaving him and his mother once again alone with their shared secret.

"So, my darling—" His mother leaned forward with the glass of red wine balanced between delicate fingers. "—is there anything in particular you want to talk about today?"

Wolfe left lunch with his mother feeling almost as on edge as when he'd sat down at the table with her. They'd talked about relationships, forming unhealthy attachments, following that particular seductive path to pleasure. Like his mother, Wolfe was a hedonist. Pleasure was his reason to live. Once something stopped feeling good, he was finished with it. And when there was something within reach that he imagined would both sate and excite him, he wanted it with a desperation that bordered on pain. Nichelle was like that for him.

He had circled around his desire for Nichelle during the conversation with his mother. And she had told him, in her own way, to take what he wanted. He wasn't sure he was ready for the consequences of that.

So, after work, he reached out for the safer option. Chantal, the woman who wanted him.

He took her to a restaurant Nichelle would never enjoy. "I'm glad you were able to meet me on such short notice," he said.

She laughed at him. "Even if you'd reached out to me an hour before, I would come. I'm very glad you called."

Wolfe watched her through the flickering candlelight on their table. She wore a pretty white dress and was beautiful, but she did not look as much like Nichelle as he first thought. There was something almost brittle about her, a desperation that seemed to have nothing to do with him and everything to do with whatever she was going through in her life. And she wasn't funny.

Nichelle had a way of laughing at the world, herself included, that he'd always found irresistible. That amusement had been there as a child but grew even more pointed, more effective, after she came back from college.

"You're very beautiful," he said to Chantal. Compliments were his usual way of putting himself back in the game when his attention wandered.

"Thank you. You are too. Beautiful that is." She blushed, and her skin, paler than Nichelle's, reddened. "I thought that when I first saw you."

"Thank you."

But that was really all the conversation they had for each other. The waitress came and left, dropping off drinks and food and pleasant enough service. It was a gourmet place, one that served small portions on pretty plates and where you left feeling as if you'd just eaten air. He toyed with his glass of whiskey and watched Chantal, carefully keeping a smile on his face.

He was usually better than this. Talking to women until their lingering unease, if there was any at all, disappeared. But despite Chantal's beauty, he wanted the date to be over. Wanted to be doing something effortless but filled to the brim with pleasure. He wanted to talk with Nichelle.

Wolfe took a long sip of his whiskey. The drink burned going down and made him think, again, of Nichelle. He wished that it was his business partner, his pretend wife, who sat on the other side of the table with a wicked eyebrow raised, daring him to be himself while heat and expectation shimmered between them like dust after a light spring rain.

The meal came, then a second round of drinks. He

found out that Chantal was an only child. That she enjoyed white water rafting, even though she couldn't swim, that her ideal vacation involved spa treatments and couples massages. Was she fishing for a relationship out of this date?

By the time they'd eaten the food and exhausted their meager small talk, Wolfe was ready to leave. But he stayed longer, drank more whiskey until the date seemed almost like a good idea.

"I like you," Chantal said, eyeing him over her third glass of champagne.

Wolfe shook his head. "You don't know me."

"But I want to."

He shook his head again, thinking about the best way to get out of Brickell and back home in his slightly drunken state. A cab. He needed to call a cab. Well, two. One for Chantal and one for himself.

"You seem so perfect," Chantal was saying. She tapped a pink-tipped fingernail against her champagne flute. "The perfect gentleman."

Wolfe grinned, feeling his teeth flash, sharklike. "You definitely don't know me."

He always treated the women he dated well. But if he wanted to sleep with them, wanted more than a date, then a little of the beast came out. He'd be growling desire into her ear by the main course, or at least flirting in a way that made her know he was thinking of taking her to bed. But he felt none of that with Chantal, so it was easy to stay the perfect, sexless gentleman.

After dinner, he called a cab, waited with her and watched her ride away in the yellow car, waving at him and smiling shyly.

Once she disappeared from sight, he got into the second cab and gave the driver an address. He was done being a perfect gentleman for the night. All evening, a pretty image had dangled in front of his eyes, making him realize what he really wanted.

It had been easy to pretend with Chantal that it was her making the blood heat in his veins, the charm surface so effortlessly while they shared their meal. But once she was gone and the date was over, he was free to be himself again. And he was free to want what he wanted. *Whom* he wanted.

He knocked on the door to the small house in Wynwood, put his hands in his pockets and waited, imagining that she was waking up in something pretty and sheer, sliding on the robe to open the door and welcome him.

"What are you doing here?"

Nichelle stood in her doorway in thin pajama pants and a T-shirt, a mirror of what Wolfe usually wore to bed. Nothing like the negligée he'd pictured. He had to laugh at himself.

"I want to talk," he said.

She made a show of looking at the skin on her wrist where she normally wore a watch. It was well past ten o'clock. "I doubt that very much." But she opened the door and let him in anyway.

Wolfe walked in, hands curled loosely in his pockets, part of him still trying to process what he was doing at Nichelle's house so late at night.

"Why have you been avoiding me?"

He followed her into the darkened living room. A sliver of light from an open doorway, her bedroom, caught his eye. Nothing else was visible in the golden light, but the fact that it was her bedroom made him painfully hard just thinking of it. Of her.

"I wasn't avoiding you," she said. "You know more than anyone how busy things have been since we took on Quraishi as a client."

She snapped on a light and stood in the middle of her pretty but efficiently designed sitting room with arms crossed.

"Tell me, really, Wolfe. Why are you here?"

She watched him with a narrowed gaze as he approached, coming even closer than he'd intended, crowding into her personal space, breathing deep to find the scent of sleep or of her bedroom nestled into the curves of her body.

"Didn't you have a date tonight?" Nichelle asked.

So she *did* know what he was doing. Not that he'd hidden his evening activities from her or from anyone. Hiding was not his style.

"Yes, I did have a date," he said. "She went home."

"And you came here." If possible, she looked even more irritated. "Why don't *you* go home?"

"Because I want to talk with you. Is there anything wrong with that?"

He stepped even closer to her. She wrinkled her nose.

"Are you drunk?"

"Buzzed. Feeling good."

An unamused smile lifted the corner of her mouth. "Don't you see the billboards? Buzzed driving is still drunk driving." She quoted the slogan with a sneer. "You could've gotten yourself arrested coming over here."

"I took a cab."

She stared at him in disbelief. The implication of his

actions occurred to him the moment her face hardened. "Get the hell out of here, Wolfe. Now."

"Stop, Nichelle." He raised his hands in surrender. "It's not like that."

"No? Then tell me that you didn't send the girl home and bring your ass over here to get some because she didn't want to put out."

"Of course she wanted to put out," he murmured with a smile. "They always do. But I want…"

"Want what?"

"I want my wife."

She drew in a sharp breath and stepped back. "No. No. You don't get to do this here. The pretense is over. Dammit—"

He kissed the next words from her mouth. Then he drifted his hands down the taut line of her back. "Nicki…" He breathed his need against her closed lips, hands on her waist, on her hips. He felt her resistance, her own hands dangling at her sides. But within the span of a heartbeat those same hands were fisting into his shirt.

"I hate you for this." And she kissed him back.

It was nothing like Morocco. Before, everything seemed like a prelude. A waiting period. Knowing that nothing would come of their touches, but wanting them anyway, savoring them. But with the release of her breath into his, the warm wet of her tongue licking his mouth, his teeth, the waiting was over.

Tonight was about taking the desire they'd shyly unfurled to each other to another level. Hunger and lust and frustration lashed between them. Wolfe was instantly sober, effortlessly throwing off that flimsy curtain of drunkenness that had given him the excuse to come to the house where the woman he wanted lived, to knock on her door and ask her things he hadn't had the courage to before.

"I want you." He breathed the words against her mouth.

She moaned and shoved into him, bit his lips. He flinched *into* her from the pain. Her hands yanked at his shirt and scattered buttons across the living room floor. He vaguely heard them bounce across the tiles, focused more on their desperate breathing, panting lust and hands on flesh, flesh against cloth, the wet sounds of their kissing.

He pressed his aching hardness into the sweet seat of her. "I want to—"

"Then do it."

Without waiting for him to do what he wanted, she shoved the shirt from his shoulders, grasping desperately at him with cool hands. She yanked his belt and fly open, slid her hand into his underwear and gripped him.

"God!"

They made it as far as the couch, Wolfe on his back, Nichelle on top, her pants discarded on the floor next to everything he'd had on.

Nichelle gasped as he mouthed his way down her throat. "I swear to God if you say tomorrow that you don't remember any of this…"

She fumbled a condom from his wallet—because his brain was too fried to remember even the simplest things—sheathed him in latex, and climbed onto him. Her wet heat sucked him in, and everything he was collapsed with the feel of her body around him. Firm clutch, tight heat, her thighs pressed to his hips. He swallowed past a rough gasp as she moved on top of him, controlling the pace.

"Wolfe." She was still. She squeezed him inside, paused to pull off her shirt.

He groaned at the sight of her small breasts and reached up to touch them. She shivered when he thumbed the firm buds of her nipples, her muscled belly rippling with reaction. Yes, he wanted this. He needed this.

She moved on top of him, a slowly rolling tide. But he wanted more. He wanted the instant explosion of it. And normally he'd be more than happy to have her control the situation, but he'd been waiting years for this moment to come. Years. And if he watched her any longer, her beautiful breasts bouncing with every movement of her on him, her wet mouth, the panting breaths that left her even more beautiful, he would lose it. He would explode, and it would all be over before it even got started.

Wolfe sat up on the couch, taking her with him. She gasped at the shifting angle, then held on to him during the stumbling, kissing and tangled fingers that comprised their journey from the living room to the bedroom. Her bed had only one side turned down, a book on the bedside table, a single lamp burning. He bore her down into the sheets without losing the hot clutch of her around him.

"I've dreamed of this for so damn long." He sank into her, even more deeply. She whimpered, her nails dragging down his back, digging into him, urging him on. "You feel so good."

Wolfe quickly lost track of what he was saying but knew that whatever it was, she liked it, her nails scoring his shoulders and flanks as they moved together on the bed. He was close already, so perilously close, but he wanted her to come first. He wanted to watch her lose control. He climbed to his knees, lifted her hips, drove into her.

She wailed. Her whole body shivered. The line of her arched neck was wet with sweat. Tears of need leaked from her closed eyes and spilled down the sides of her face and onto his tongue. She was so beautiful. He loved her harder, filling her with his heat, every inch of his pleasure. His body quivered from the feel of her, hot and humid around him, pulling him deeper, squeezing him. Pulling him closer and closer to explosion.

She cried out his name. A plea. The scent of sweat and their sex rose up around him. Wolfe pressed his thumb on the hot little button while his hips snapped into hers. She fell apart around him, screaming, shuddering into him.

The hot clasp of her destroyed the rest of his self-control. One moment, he was watching the frantic breath and heaving breasts. Her teeth anchored in her swollen lips, the agony of lust on her face. And the next he was growling out his own orgasm, jerking viciously as his body emptied into her.

His eyes rolled back in his head, and he slumped heavily over her, frozen in that instant of indescribable bliss. Spent. Under him, she panted softly, blinking sweat from her eyes. She was so damned beautiful, he almost didn't deserve her.

Wolfe pressed a kiss under her ear, down the damp line of her throat. She murmured something he lost in the still pounding rush of blood through his body. But he gathered her tenderly through all that, settled her into the bed. And kissed her again. She sighed into his mouth and her arms draped down his neck, still trembling.

His body was spent for the night. But he wanted to please her more, to give her even a fraction of the spine-melting pleasure she'd gifted to him.

How could he have gotten this lucky to have her? He kissed down her body, pausing at each rise of flesh to lick and suck, stroke and hum his enjoyment. She moaned softly. Then gasped when he settled between her thighs. She was tender there, slightly swollen from where he had loved her. He kissed the delicate flesh. She sighed, fingers sliding over his head, alighting on his neck, his shoulders.

She smelled like perfection, like sex and fulfillment. A combination to him that usually signaled the end of the evening. But now his mouth watered for a taste of what he'd only touched before. He licked her. She gasped, trembled, her thighs pressing wide open.

He smiled against her flesh at the greediness of her action. Much of her personality translated to how she was in bed, nakedly wanting, desiring and going after what she wanted. Her nails dug into his shoulders, into the back of his neck to push him deeper into her damp center. She wanted him and wasn't afraid to let him know.

He burrowed into the tight, seafoam-scented wet of her, and she gave him the slick of her arousal, her stuttering moans, the wild flex of her thighs around his head. The mattress heaved with the rough toss of her body. She writhed under him as he loved her with his mouth, teased her wetness, the firm pearl of her clitoris, skimmed with his curled fingers the space inside of her that made her shout out his name.

"Wolfe!" Her sharp demand cut his teasing off at the knees.

He stopped playing and latched his lips to the firm bud, slid his fingers deep, lashed her with his tongue, hummed into her hot flesh.

"God. Yes! Please. Yes. More…"

She moaned as if in pain, her hips circling in the bed, curling up into his face, the circles growing tighter and more frantic the more he thrust his fingers, fluttered his tongue. She cried out again, his name a screaming wail. But he still didn't stop.

Her nails dug into his shoulders again, deeper. Another tremor quaked through her, thighs vibrating. Then another and another. Wailing cries and pleas. She pressed the heels of her hands into her eyes as she cried out still, her hips bucking and wild beneath the steely grip of his hands.

"More," she moaned.

And he gave it to her. Fingers, his tongue, until his body was firm again, and he pulled her up in the bed, bent her over the pillows and took her until she screamed in satisfaction again and again. He exploded with her, an electric current. They collapsed together into the sheets, gasping, damp flesh sliding together.

He gathered her into his arms and rolled to one side of the massive bed. A sound of contentment purred from her, then she became a limp weight on top of him. Asleep. His own eyes drooped, his lust satisfied, his woman put to sleep, but he glanced down at himself sleepily, pulled off the condom and slid from beneath her to go to the bathroom. She made a soft noise but didn't move.

When he got back to the bed, she was right where he left her. He curled protectively around her soft and scented weight and draped a hand over her hip. He fell asleep to the thought that he could very well get used to this, falling asleep next to his very own wife.

Nichelle opened her eyes to the pale light of dawn. She stretched in her bed, sighing into the feeling of satisfaction and contentment. The hard warmth at her back felt completely natural, something she'd wanted for so long that it didn't register as strange until a deep voice groaned in sleepy protest and firm hands settled on her hips to pull her closer.

She blinked and slowly turned to face the man in her bed. It hadn't been a dream. He was as beautiful as she'd always known he would be, stretched out on her pale linens, his lashes resting on his high cheekbones, mouth slack in sleep. He breathed deeply and easily as he slept, in contrast to the way her own breath sped up, her pulse knocking frantically in her neck.

Oh my God...

She slid from the bed, her knees trembling as she stared down at the beautiful man spread out on her sheets.

What the...?

She stumbled to the bathroom and snapped on the light. In the mirror, she saw she was a wreck, mouth still swollen, her neck and chest dotted with love bites, her eyes drowsy with satisfaction. Probably looked just like any other woman Wolfe had been with.

She didn't want to be one of them. Screwed today,

tossed out tomorrow. And she didn't want to ruin what she and Wolfe had at the firm. But now, they could no longer go back to what they had been. It was impossible. The thought made her slump against the sink, her arms trembling from holding up her weight.

She needed to leave.

Nichelle shook herself into motion, quickly got dressed in what was sitting on top of the laundry hamper—sweat pants and a tank top—and left the bathroom then the house. In the car, she grabbed her phone and redialed the last number she'd called the night before.

Barely half an hour later, she walked into Novlette's café, one of her favorite coffee and brunch places. She grabbed a salted caramel latte and almond croissant at the front counter before heading out to the terrace to search for Nala. Nichelle found her at one of the little French café-style tables, her hands clasped around a coffee cup, head down.

Nichelle shoved the croissant toward her friend, then sat in the empty seat across from her in silence while the sun struggled for the horizon.

"Thanks for meeting me," she croaked. "I just had to talk to you." Nichelle swallowed around the thick lump in her throat.

"I can't believe you dragged me out at ass crack of morning and expect actual coherent conversation." Nala held her cup of coffee under her nose, sniffed the rising steam but did not drink. She barely glanced at the pastry Nichelle brought her.

Her hair was scraped back from her face with a steel headband, a black cat suit hugged her body and a red cropped top drooped from one shoulder.

"You've dragged me out of my house for worse," Nichelle muttered.

They'd remained friends through much drama, including the time in high school when the girl Nala was dating also tried to get under Nichelle's boyfriend at the time. One school fight and countless ride-or-die sidekick missions later, neither woman was going anywhere.

Nala chuckled, beginning to wake up over her coffee. "Oh my God, remember that time when—"

"Nichelle, how nice to see you."

A man unexpectedly appeared over Nala's shoulder.

"Good morning, Isaac." She greeted him with her most civil smile. What the hell was he doing on the East Coast?

Nala turned around, gave him the once over, then dismissed him in favor of sniffing more of her coffee. Nichelle sipped hers. Maybe she wasn't awake enough for this, either.

Isaac looked disgustingly well-rested, ready for the day in boat shoes, pressed khakis and a white dress shirt rolled up to the elbows. He carried a cardboard to-go tray with three large coffees.

"I see you're not wearing your pretty sparkler these days." He nodded toward her ring finger. When she realized she was rubbing the bare spot on her finger with her thumb, she stopped the motion. It had taken her days to get used to its absence. And now with just a few words, Isaac made her aware again of how naked her finger felt without that reminder of Wolfe wrapped around it.

"I see that your eyes are working." She tipped her head over her shoulder to see a car idling near them in the parking lot. Then she turned back to pointedly look at him. "It was interesting running into you, Isaac. Please don't make a habit of it." Then she turned back to Nala. "I could go for a walk," she said to her friend. "How about you?"

"Screw that. I just sat down. We can go for a walk when there's more sun and I'm in a better mood."

When Isaac didn't leave, Nala showed him a finger that also didn't have a ring on it. "My sparkler is at the jeweler's," she said with a smirk.

He said something under his breath about immature women and strode away toward the car waiting for him.

"Was he an ass, or is it me?"

"I think it's a tie," Nichelle muttered.

Nala laughed and choked on her coffee. "Bitch."

The sun gradually rolled higher in the sky above them, spreading its warm light over the terrace where they sat. With the rising sun came Nala's coherence and better mood. She poked at the croissant in front of her.

"So, from this random outfit, am I to assume you just rolled out of a bed not your own?"

"It was my bed, but I left Wolfe in it."

Nala's mouth dropped open. "So you finally got some of that?"

"You make it sound like I've been waiting forever to screw my business partner."

"Weren't you?"

She flushed, aware there was some truth to the question, the desire she'd harbored for longer than she'd even been aware of. "Shut up." She sipped her lukewarm coffee and wrinkled her nose at the taste. "I wasn't planning for it to happen. He came to my house after a date."

"A date?" Nala choked on her laughter, shaking her head as if the idea of him leaving another woman to climb into Nichelle's bed was awful but also awfully hilarious. "Are you serious?"

"That's pretty much what I said when he walked in my door."

"And you let him through your door...?"

She blushed again. But it was true. As if she could ever turn him away. "I did. But it was incredibly stupid. He can get sex from just about any woman on the planet. Why the hell did I allow him in my house last night?"

"Because you wanted to. It's been a long time, Nicki." Nala held up eight fingers, ticking them off one by one as she listed all the months since Nichelle had had a man in her bed.

"I wasn't starved for it."

"So you say, but if not, why jump on Wolfe?"

"Because..." But she didn't have a reason beyond her desperate and sudden yearning for him.

Every woman wanted Wolfe. But what good did that do them? He loved women, but they tumbled so cheerfully and easily into his bed that he took them for granted. All of them. He easily moved on to the next one because there would always be a next.

And last night, she felt as if she'd been easy for him. The week in Marrakesh had teased them both with the possibility of how intimacy would be between them. In some ways, she could have even justified sleeping with him there. But here, in Miami, for Wolfe, making love with her had been convenient, a novelty that would wear off with the coming of the morning sun.

Nichelle cursed. "I feel like such an idiot."

Nala waved a dismissive hand. "Stop beating yourself up. It was only sex. And sex that you both wanted.

It wasn't like you raped him or destroyed the whole world with the force of your orgasm."

"Orgasms," Nichelle corrected. She shoved her coffee cup against her mouth to stop herself from saying anything else. But that didn't stop her thoughts from stuttering back to hours before, her body arched in the bed under the force of Wolfe's merciless tongue and fingers, while she cried out for him to stop, but *not* stop, what he was doing.

Nala chortled. "And you have regrets about this one? Damn, you should have regretted that boring University of Miami professor with the tiny penis. Now that was a waste of your three minutes."

Her comment teased a smile out of Nichelle. She agreed with Nala. The decision to let the professor go had been an easy one. Wolfe and his magical mouth and hands, not so much. But she had to let him go before he dropped her like he had so many of the others before her.

"I can't let him hurt me, Nala. I just can't."

"Who's to say that he will? You're assuming an awful lot, friend."

"I'm not assuming. I'm inferring based on the behavior I've observed over the years." Nichelle toyed with the handle of her cup. "I can't do this with him. It's not going to end well, and I won't allow him to treat me like the others who ended up falling for him."

Nala plucked apart her almond croissant, finger-painted the nutty filling across the plate and licked her thumb. "I never realized before what a pessimist you are, Nichelle. You're throwing away something sweet.

But I'll be here for you when you regret it and need a shoulder to cry on."

"That won't happen," Nichelle said.

But even to her, the words sounded empty and false.

Chapter 11

Wolfe woke up alone in Nichelle's bed.

He opened his eyes and blinked around the unfamiliar room. No, not unfamiliar. He'd seen this bedroom before, but had never been in the bed and certainly not naked. He sat up and called out Nichelle's name.

But the house was quiet. He glanced by reflex to the bedside table, expecting…something. But there was no note, certainly no breakfast and no other sound in the house except the softly humming air conditioner. The bedroom door was closed. He'd never woken up alone in someone else's bed before. He'd thought he and Nichelle would—

He scrubbed a hand over his face. He wasn't sure what he thought.

Wolfe took a breath and jumped from the bed. He couldn't stand being there anymore. He got dressed and left the house, locking the front door behind him. Sex with Nichelle was supposed to be about pleasure and enjoying the uncomplicated joy of their bodies. This part wasn't fun, though—waking up alone under the weight of his crushed expectations and wondering why she'd left. This role reversal was a bitch.

The day after Nichelle left him in her bed, Wolfe was still feeling hollowed out by the aftermath of his night with her. But this time, he blamed himself. He had wanted her, and so he took, without regard for the potential consequences of his actions. The bittersweet memory of her, warm and clutching around him, haunted him from his sprawl on the back terrace of his Coconut Grove house. The rising sun threw its faint light across the backyard and through the rippling waters of the pool.

The night with her had exceeded every fantasy. She'd touched him and welcomed him into her body in ways that both shocked and pleased him. Her soft mouth and hands, the sweetness of her most intimate flesh pulling him toward bliss. And then to see even more of her cool facade melt away in the wake of their passion had been humbling. And sexy as hell.

Wolfe dropped his head back and hissed, hands tightening on his thighs, his body hard already from the memory of having her and wanting her again. His drunkenness had been no excuse. He didn't want any excuses made for taking what he had desired for so long. But he knew things were different now. Every good thing between them had been destroyed.

His phone vibrated on the table in front of him, tapping a harsh rhythm against the glass top. He didn't look at it. A few seconds later, it rang again. He turned it over just as a text from his mother came through.

I'm coming in. Get dressed if you're indecent.

Wolfe looked down at himself. Bare chest, cotton pajama bottoms. Decent enough. When she let herself into the house barely two minutes later, he already had the kettle on and was reaching into his cupboard for her favorite tea, a Japanese concoction that cost a small fortune.

"Good morning, darling." She brought the smell of pumpkin-spice coffee with her. When she saw him, she paused in the doorway. "You look like hell."

"Is that why you came over here so early, to shower me with compliments?"

She sailed into the open-plan dining room and kitchen, looking much too lively for six o'clock in the morning, and carrying a large cup of coffee held out like a peace offering. Her yellow dress was a burst of sunshine in the dawn-shrouded room. She frowned and touched his cheek, fingers rasping through his overnight whiskers.

"You look like you've overindulged," she said.

Still feeling raw and not exactly ready to be civil to another human, Wolfe carefully stepped away from her touch. "I *don't* have a hangover."

"I didn't say anything about a hangover. You, my son, look like regret."

She put the coffee on the bar and uncapped it to release the aromatic trail of steam. The smell of pumpkin spice became even stronger, perking up Wolfe's taste buds. She must have stopped by one of the few places in all of Miami that served pumpkin-spice coffee, his secret pleasure, all year long. He reached for the cup.

"Sometimes you want something very badly," his mother murmured, almost meditatively. "When you take it, it's good. So good that you wonder why you'd never taken it before, and you want to keep having it. But you can't. That's the regret I see in you."

Wolfe stopped at the bar with his hands braced on either side of the open coffee cup. He put them into fists and closed his eyes, sickened suddenly by the coffee smell.

"I'm not like you," he said. But because his words sounded weak and unconvincing, he said them louder, slamming his fist against the granite counter. "I'm *not* like you!"

In the kitchen, the kettle screamed. They both ignored it.

His mother arranged herself on a bar stool, draping the hem of her dress carefully over her legs. "What happened to you, darling?"

Was she even listening to him? "Shi—!"

"Do not curse in front of your mother, Wolfe Forsythe Diallo." She didn't even have to raise her voice.

He clamped his mouth shut but could not look at her. The tangled emotions, the frustration, bubbled in him like acid. The kettle's hysterical scream wasn't helping matters. In the kitchen, he snapped off the flame and moved the kettle to a cold burner. The sudden silence between them was even louder.

"When you left us sixteen years ago, I thought my life as I knew it was over." Wolfe stepped back from the stove and into the dining area, hands on his hips so he wouldn't be tempted to hit something again. "I thought that was the worst of it, you know. You leaving and taking every ounce of joy in our house with you."

He took a harsh breath, and the feelings from that long ago cool Miami afternoon rushed back to punch him in the chest. "But I was wrong about that day. The worst of it was when I realized I was like you." He gritted his teeth to stop the shout of anger and disappointment rising up in his throat. "Like you, I crushed one of the best things I'd ever had just because I couldn't keep it in my pants." He finally turned to face his mother. "I slept with Nichelle."

Her reaction wasn't quite what he'd thought it would be. "It's about damn time," she said.

"No, I don't think you heard me. I just ruined one of the best relationships I've ever had. She told me to back off, but I just wouldn't leave well enough alone."

"You've been dancing around each other for years now." His mother rapped her fingers against the bar's granite surface for emphasis. "Everyone can see you're perfect for each other. Even Kingsley, your own brother, has been baiting you so you'd step in and challenge him for her."

As if that would even be a challenge. Wolfe ignored the thought. "No. It's not like that." He ground his teeth together, frustrated again by his inability to think clearly where Nichelle was concerned. "She is everything to me."

The words surprised him. He gasped softly as the truth of them tumbled over him. "But I'd rather have her as a business partner, the way things were, than how they are now. I honestly think that she hates me. She left me alone in her bed, for Christ's sake."

"Listen." She held up a hand to stall him. "Before you slept with her, did you tell her how you feel?"

He grunted, a dismissive sound. "That would have

had her running for the hills for sure." Wolfe didn't want their relationship to linger on in its platonic limbo, but he didn't want to lose her, either.

"You don't know that she would run," his mother said.

He turned his back to her, head dropping low, footsteps taking him toward the open doors of the terrace. "Mother..."

"Wolfe. I didn't raise a coward. I didn't raise a carbon copy of myself, either. Because you were so busy avoiding being me, you've always taken the path to easy happiness. But without risks, my darling boy, there can be no blissful forever."

His mother pressed her lips together, hopped from the bar stool and paced to the kitchen to make her tea. She created a slow ceremony of scooping the right amount of tea leaves into the round infuser and pouring the hot water and agave into the clear teacup, then a slice of ginger. She was stalling. Which seemed so absolutely wrong because his mother *never* paused, *never* stalled. Instead she always rushed headlong into whatever decision she made, damn the consequences.

Finally, after the tea was made to her satisfaction, or she had delayed as much as she could get away with, she met his gaze.

"The weeks up until I left your father, I was in the middle of the worst postpartum depression I'd ever been through."

He flinched in surprise. *Depression?* The strongest woman he'd ever known?

"I was crying all the time," his mother continued. "Home began to feel like a prison. All those needy children plus the newborn twins made me want to do something drastic, something…awful."

Wolfe's stomach tightened. He swallowed the sudden lump in his throat. He'd read some terrible things about women dealing with postpartum depression, how they'd killed themselves or their children. Sometimes both.

His mother lifted the tea to her mouth, held the steaming cup under her nose. She stood in his kitchen, surrounded by stainless steel, a softness that he'd never seen from her before emerging as if by painful alchemy. It was an unfamiliar tableau.

"Royce, the man I left my family for, appeared at a time when I needed the distraction. I never loved him, but he saved me from myself. Sometimes I like to think he saved my family, too." She paused and sipped the hot tea, flinching from where it must have burned her lips, but she took another sip. "With him in Vanuatu, I let everything go. That distance gave me the clarity and strength I needed. When your father came to get me, it was because I called him. I was ready to come home and be with my children and husband again. I don't call myself a saint. I enjoyed Royce's body…" Wolfe flinched again. He wasn't ready to hear any of that about his mother. "And I enjoyed the sunshine and sea water on my skin. But that was the reason I left. To wash away the scum of depression that had formed over my life. I had three sets of twins, teenagers, newborns. Even with your father being there and being wonderful, it was still too much."

"I don't know why you two had so many damn kids in the first place." Wolfe tried to make light of it, although his hands were cold from the shock of her confession.

"That's what we both wanted and agreed to. Honestly, your father and I didn't know what we were setting ourselves up for." A twisted version of a smile tugged at her mouth. She was slowly becoming herself again.

"So what you're saying to me, then, is that I've been wrong about what happened for all these years?"

"You were a child, Wolfe. I didn't expect you to understand adult things." Her mouth tilted up. "Nor did I owe you any explanations. My husband understood."

"But… I spent so many years hating you."

"And yourself, too, apparently."

Heat flooded the back of Wolfe's neck. He scratched at his nape, unable to meet her gaze. "I don't hate myself."

"But you're not giving yourself what you need, either." His mother gave him a pitying look. "Making love to Nichelle was not an act of selfishness. From now on, what *you* do will determine the ultimate meaning of Friday night. Don't treat her like she's nothing. Let her know that what you experienced together can be worth more than the deal you two just closed on. Emotionally, that is."

Wolfe shook his head. "How do you know that?"

"Because I know my son." She passed him on the way out to the terrace. "Now grab your coffee and come sit out here with me. Let's not waste this beautiful sunrise."

Because he was a good son, he did what she told him, the words of their conversation ringing in his ears. Slowly, he relaxed, his tight shoulders loosening, the pressure in his chest nearly gone. Wolfe sat across the table from her and put his bare feet up next to hers in the same empty chair. He lifted his cup.

"Thanks for bringing the coffee."

She smiled around the lip of the teacup, her eyes warm and golden brown in the thickening light. "Anytime."

Monday morning, Wolfe walked into the office just after eight o'clock, eager to talk with Nichelle. He rounded a corner in time to see her back disappearing down the hallway. He buttoned his suit jacket, took a breath and walked quickly after her.

"Good morning, Nichelle."

She stopped. Her gaze dropped to his tie, the green silk paisley she'd bought him years ago for their first business trip together, and she smiled, a barely there tug at the corners of her mouth. Although she stood just a few feet from him, she felt as distant as the moon.

"Hi." Nichelle reached out to touch the tie, then caught herself, dropping her hand back to her side. She cleared her throat. "I was expecting you earlier. The strategy meeting is just about to start."

Wolfe glanced at his watch, annoyed that he wouldn't get to talk with her. "Who the hell scheduled a meeting so damn early in the morning?"

"You did," she said serenely. "I've got to grab some papers from my office. Meet you in the conference room."

Then she was walking away again. Back straight under a pale yellow blouse tucked into a black skirt. Her shoes were also yellow today. Their red soles flashed at him with each step, signaling both danger and desire. He wanted to follow but knew it was a bad idea.

How often had women come up to him after a memorable night asking why he'd left or hadn't called for a second date? The flipped script was grating on his nerves *and* his pride, only made worse by the fact that it was Nichelle doing it. But if she knew that the night had been about more than satisfying a temporary itch, would she turn to him in welcome? Or would she walk away even faster? Maybe his mother *had* raised a coward.

Damn.

Wolfe looked at his watch again. He didn't have time to moon over Nichelle like some punany-struck teenager. There were notes he had to look over for the forgotten meeting. He strode quickly toward his office.

Despite the disaster of his forgetfulness, the strategy meeting went off without a hitch. The room of Kingston executives even came up with workable solutions to the potential problems Nichelle saw on the horizon.

He left the meeting split in two. His mind was on the strategies he needed to begin implementing on his end. Everything else was fiercely focused on Nichelle and the way the yellow blouse looked over her summer-ripe skin. How, during the meeting, she had stroked a pen against her lips in thought, tapping the shiny black pen against the plump red of her mouth in a steady rhythm that echoed in his groin. He could swear his flesh was still imprinted with the shape of her kisses, lust bites on his throat and chest, her teeth marks on his belly.

Wolfe had to pull himself together before he was able to stand up from the conference table. He immediately went to find Nichelle. He rapped on her office door once before pushing it open.

"Hey."

She sat at her desk, fingers poised on her computer keyboard.

"Hey." She smiled back at him, but had that same distant look, her eyes a dark ocean he had no chance of sailing safely through. "What's going on?" she asked.

"About Friday night…" Wolfe closed her office door behind him. He didn't miss the slight tightening of her shoulders at his approach. He stopped, shoved his hands in his pockets and gave her the space she so obviously wanted.

"We're okay," she said, dismissive and calm. "You needed a little something, and I was there. No big deal."

No big deal? The pleasure he'd shared with her far eclipsed any he'd had with any other woman. It had only been one night, but he wanted more. He wanted *her.*

Nichelle took a deep breath and put down her pen. She clasped her hands together on the desk. "This doesn't need to go any further, Wolfe. Really."

"And that's all you want to say about this?" *It can't be.* The thought pulsed in him, hard and painful. After the things they'd shared in Morocco and the way she responded with him in bed, this couldn't be the end.

"Yes, it is."

She tapped the keyboard, obviously ready to get back to work. Dismissing him. But a flicker of something unfamiliar in her eyes caught him. She was…afraid. Then the fear was gone, and it was just Nichelle staring at him with an upraised brow. Whatever she was feeling, she didn't want him to see it. He had to respect that.

"Okay." He nodded. "I have a lunch meeting in Fort Lauderdale. I'm heading that way now."

"Sounds good. See you when you get back." She turned back to her computer.

Wolfe's lips tightened. But he let himself out and closed her door very deliberately behind him. This was going to be a long, damned day.

Nichelle kept her eyes on the computer for a full thirty seconds after Wolfe walked out of her office, only blinking, unseeing, at the screen. Regret, a spiked and hard thing, rolled through her chest. She clenched her teeth to prevent the words that would call Wolfe back to her. He'd looked so hurt. Maybe there was a way they could—

The telephone rang, derailing her train of thought. Was it Wolfe calling?

But it was her assistant's voice that came over the line. "There's an Isaac Franklin on the phone for you, Ms. Wright."

What would he want to talk to her about? She pursed her lips, considering. "Put him through, please."

"I know what you did to get the Quraishi account." Isaac didn't bother with any pleasantries.

Nichelle hissed an indrawn breath, then forced herself to stay calm. Isaac was a bully and not very smart. What he thought might be dirt on her and Wolfe might actually be nothing. "What do you mean? That I had the best proposal, better resources, and was more prepared to do my job than you?" She leaned back at her desk, consciously relaxing her body.

"The two of you were pretending to be married to impress Quraishi. You took advantage of his conservative stance to push your proposal through."

"What he may or may not think about my personal life with Wolfe has no bearing on the job we'll do for him as his business management consultants." She gave him the party line, hoping he'd give up and get off her phone.

"If Quraishi knew you two played him, he would snatch that account from Kingston Consulting so damn fast you'd get whiplash."

Nichelle tapped her fingers against the desk, already mentally doing damage control. "What's the point of this call, Isaac? What do you want?"

"You know what I want."

"To grow a few more inches?" She was deliberately nasty, adding a sneer in her voice. She wished he was standing in front of her so she could stare witheringly at his crotch for maximum effect.

"You're going to tell Quraishi everything," Isaac said. "*Or* you drop Diallo and come back to work for us. If you come back to Sterling, I won't say a word to Quraishi."

And by leaving Kingston, she was as good as telling Quraishi she'd lied anyway. What wife would abandon her husband and his business to work for a mediocre competitor? Not a very smart one. "Why the hell would I do any of that?"

"If you care anything for Diallo and his company, why wouldn't you?" Then he hung up.

Nichelle glared at the silent telephone as anger knocked an erratic pulse in her throat, and she pressed her teeth viciously together. She wanted to find Isaac wherever he was in Miami and gut him like the useless bottom-feeder he was. She buzzed her assistant instead.

"Isaac Franklin doesn't get through to me again."

"Yes, ma'am. Understood."

Nichelle disconnected the call, only to have her cell phone chime a second later. It was a text from Nala inviting her out to lunch. She texted back: I can't. Something came up at work. Dinner tonight?

A minute later Nala wrote back: Fine. But you're buying. Romeo's Café.

A brief smile quirked Nichelle's mouth. Her friend *would* pick one of the most expensive restaurants in Miami in retaliation for Nichelle not being available when she wanted. She texted: Fine. But you're picking me up.

Nala: You're on.

She put the phone down, already thinking again of Isaac and the threats he made. She had to find a way to fix this. No matter what was going on between her and Wolfe, she wouldn't allow someone else to hurt him. But her usually quick mental reflexes couldn't find a solution to the conundrum Isaac had left her with. She could only sit in the chair, frozen, remembering Wolfe's face only minutes before when she'd basically told him to leave her alone. That had hurt his feelings, but Isaac Franklin had the power to cripple his business.

Nichelle's hand clenched into a fist.

Wolfe maneuvered his sleek burgundy Mercedes-Benz through downtown Fort Lauderdale while 2 Chainz growled from the car's speakers. His meeting had gone well, another guaranteed win for Kingston Consulting, but dissatisfaction writhed under his skin. He couldn't get Nichelle out of his mind. Not the way she dismissed him that morning, not the way she had felt moving beneath him as they'd made love only days before.

The music in the car faded to nothing when his phone started to ring. A photo of Nichelle appeared on the screen of his cell, a picture he'd taken of her at a family dinner. Velvet eyes smiling, her mouth bare of lipstick, a peacock-blue dress making her skin look like black gold. She was so breathtakingly beautiful.

A car horn honked sharply behind him, jerking his attention back to the road and the green light he was currently wasting. He set the car back in motion the same time the phone stopped ringing.

He lifted his thumb to hit the redial button when the phone rang again.

"Good, I'm glad you called back."

"Are you sure you're talking to the right person?"

The masculine voice at the other end of the line made him glance at the caller ID he'd ignored before. An unknown local number. But his brain caught up and he recognized the voice.

"Isaac Franklin."

"Got it in one."

"I didn't know we were playing guessing games."

Franklin laughed, but there was no humor in it. "I just talked to your wife."

"I don't have a wife," Wolfe said before he could stop himself.

"That's not what Quraishi thinks."

Wolfe sucked in a silent breath. "What he may or may not think is none of your business. In case you already forgot, he's not your client. He's ours."

"In case *you* forgot, you told him a lie to get the contract. He wouldn't take very kindly to knowing that."

"Get the hell off my line, Franklin." He hung up.

Wolfe was getting off on the exit toward Coral Gables, passing the airport with planes taking off low overhead, when his phone rang again, from another line he had forwarded to his cell. The phone number plainly said it was from California. It had to be Franklin again. Despite the unease in his gut, he answered the call.

"Whatever you have to say, make it quick," he growled into the phone.

"You may not know Nichelle as well as you think, Diallo." Franklin sounded smug. "I know what you two got up to in Morocco." Had he watched them from the tent while they'd pressed together under the desert stars? No. Franklin wasn't talking about that.

"She's beautiful, isn't she?" Franklin continued. "That heart-shaped mole on her hip is like a stamp of perfection. They don't make them like that anymore."

A cold shiver raked through Wolfe. He'd never seen the mole until the night he and Nichelle made love. It was an inky beauty mark near the seat of her sex that he'd licked and bit until she gasped his name, begged him to move his mouth lower. Bile rose in his throat at the thought of Franklin touching it.

"You've never been that lucky in your life," Wolfe rumbled. He slammed on the brakes when he almost rear-ended the car in front of him.

"I *have* been that lucky," Franklin said. "And could have been again if a man higher up on the food chain hadn't come along for her to sink her claws into."

Wolfe remembered their night together, her nails raking his shoulders and back, the sharp tips digging into his skin, bringing him unbearable pleasure mixed with pain. The images rampaging through his head struck him dumb, made him grip and release his hand around the steering wheel.

"You need to realize that she's all for herself. She's going to leave you and Kingston Consulting and take the Quraishi contract with her. Watch her carefully and see. I didn't pay attention to my own advice, and she damn near crushed me."

"She never slept with you," Wolfe finally hissed.

"Is that what she told you?"

The indistinct sounds of conversation came through the phone, a jarring noise given the absolute quiet of moments before. Franklin was on the move.

"Good luck with that viper, Diallo. I'm just telling you the score before you become another one of her victims. It's not a good look on any man."

Wolfe hung up, clenching his jaw so hard it hurt. He looked around, saw that he had driven on autopilot back to the office and he sat in the parking lot, listening to the music that had pulsed back on once the call ended. Anger churned in his belly. He silenced the speakers.

Franklin was a liar. There was nothing he could tell Wolfe about Nichelle that he would believe. Certainly no ridiculous story about her stooping low enough to sleep with a colleague to advance her career. But the echoing silence in the car was haunting. A chill washed over him. He needed to talk with her. Now.

But when he got back into the building, Nichelle wasn't there. Wolfe hesitated in the open door of her office, the specter of their Friday night encounter haunting him even more than what Franklin said. She'd left him alone in her bed, for God's sake!

It looked as if she had packed up for the day, the computer shut down, her purse gone. He sat down behind her desk and leaned back in her chair, fitting his body to the same contours she did nearly every day.

Okay, this is getting creepy.

Wolfe started to get up when an envelope, propped

on the footrest under the desk, drew his attention. He plucked it from its perch—and drew a surprised breath. The envelope was from Sterling Solutions and stamped "private." There was nothing inside it. What the hell did this mean? He thought back to Franklin's phone call.

"No." *No way.*

He dropped the empty envelope on Nichelle's desk as if it were on fire and turned, nearly stumbling on a floor lamp, to make his way to his own office. A reminder on his phone beeped.

Family dinner tonight.

He'd forgotten all about it, which was the purpose of reminders, he thought with a wry twist of his mouth. With effort, he pushed the Sterling envelope from his mind and called his mother as soon as he got back to his desk.

"Dinner is still on for tonight?"

"Of course. When do I cancel something this important at the last minute?" The answer was never. She treasured the family dinners perhaps more than anyone, proof and celebration that she still had a family despite everything that had happened years before. "Bring a bottle or two of your favorite red wine. Your father asked for steak tonight, but our last party sucked up the last of our good wine."

"Yes, ma'am."

"You're such a good son." She laughed. "See you tonight."

Hours later, freshly showered and shaved, he rang his parents' doorbell. Nala opened the door. He automatically looked behind her, searching for Nichelle.

"Why are you ringing your own doorbell?"

"Mama will be the first to tell you that this doorbell

is definitely not mine." He greeted her with a brief kiss to the cheek, then walked past her with a carton of wine under his arm. The bottles clinked in the box as he put them down to give her a proper hug. "Besides, the times I walked in on something I didn't want to see as a kid made the practice of ringing a doorbell and knocking once or twice the rule rather than the exception."

Jealousy flashed briefly across Nala's face. Even before her parents died and left her alone, they'd never been as close or as passionate as his own. He squeezed her waist in sympathy.

"You on your own tonight?"

"Nope." Nala gave him a knowing look, the jealousy gone from her face as if it had never been. "Nicki is upstairs. Chatting with your father, I think."

She's here. Okay. He took a deep breath. "Cool."

The house was already lively with conversation and music, Toots and the Maytals playing from the stereo, two sets of twins smack talking over a game of spades in the sitting room. Sounds of a playful disagreement drifted down at him from upstairs.

He found his mother in the kitchen, laughing with his sister Alice and maneuvering a large casserole dish, steaming with the scents of broccoli and cheese, to the large center island.

"Wolfe." She shucked off the potholders to hug him and kiss his cheek. The mingled scents of cooking food—steak, garlic sautéed vegetables, rosemary potatoes—made his mouth water.

"Hey, Mama." He gave her a long and tight hug, then pulled back to smile into her eyes. "Where's Daddy?"

"In the den. Jaxon is trying to convince him to buy some new gadget or other."

"So he can inherit it after Daddy gets frustrated with trying to learn the new tech?"

"Exactly."

Wolfe laughed. "Some things never change."

He greeted everyone else he found lingering in the kitchen, before wandering off to find his father. In the den, his father sat at his desk, the computer on, and Jaxon, half of the youngest set of three twins, perched on the edge talking about terabytes and hardware upgrades.

Wolfe stopped when he noticed Nichelle on the other side of the desk, her arms loosely crossed over her stomach while she nodded in response to something his older brother, Kingsley, was saying. She was wearing a houndstooth check dress tonight, the black-and-white fabric hugging her body from collar to knees. Wolfe's gaze drifted to her hands, over her bare wedding ring finger where he'd grown used to seeing that flare of yellow fire.

Nichelle glanced at him then, a flash of her long-lashed gaze lingering on him before turning back to his brother. He shook off his stupor and went over to his father, squeezed his shoulder. "Daddy."

"My boy!"

His father shoved away from the desk, and from Jaxon's look of annoyance at being interrupted, to embrace Wolfe in a giant, breath-stealing hug.

Maybe I need to visit home more often, Wolfe thought. "Is this one trying to get you to spend more money on crap that's going to be obsolete in six months?"

His father chuckled, a deep rumble in his wide chest. "Something like that."

"Keep your opinions to yourself, Wolfe," Jaxon said. "You don't know a damn thing about tech." His brother, a nineteen-year-old who knew everything, was only half teasing.

"I know enough to realize when spending money is a waste."

"Aren't you a millionaire or something? Why are you here counting somebody else's pennies? Look out for your own business." He jerked his chin toward Nichelle, who laughed while Kingsley stepped closer to touch her shoulder much too intimately.

Wolfe told his brother what he could do with his opinion.

"You first." Jaxon grinned.

"None of that talk around here, boys. If your mother caught you, she'd give me hell for it." His father sat again at the desk and waved toward his youngest son. "If you think this thing isn't a waste, show us what you're about."

Jaxon grinned at the challenge and hunkered even closer to the large computer screen, gripping the mouse. "Okay, take a look at this…"

Wolfe stopped paying attention to his brother. Instead, he listened to the conversation Nichelle was having with Kingsley, a conversation that seemed intimate despite the very public atmosphere of the den.

Nichelle's voice was low and interested as she talked with his brother. Kingsley said something to her about the new account with Quraishi Industries, about her possibly moving on to another firm. She shrugged, but didn't say anything about staying.

"Business is always changing," she said. "For better or worse. The people you align with today might be your enemy tomorrow or vice versa."

"That's true," he said. "But what about doing something more for yourself? Building your own firm, branching out and taking the initiative, grabbing another challenging project?"

"Why? Are you trying to make me an offer I can't refuse?"

Kingsley laughed, the dimples flashing in his cheeks. "I don't think I have that much money at my disposal. At least not yet. But I'm really envious of what my brother did with your help. I don't think he could have come this far without you."

"Envy is a fine enough emotion," she said, her mouth red and moist in the soft lamplight. "But your brother worked hard for what he has, separate from me, and you would have to, as well."

"Damn, I know that but—"

Wolfe had had enough. "Hey." He drifted over to them, brushed a hand over Nichelle's shoulder. "Can we talk for a minute?"

Did he imagine it, or had she closed her eyes just the tiniest bit at his touch?

Kingsley bristled. "We're discussing something important here." He gave Wolfe a narrow-eyed stare. His brother had grown up alongside Wolfe to notice how beautiful Nichelle was, even though Wolfe had been telling Kingsley for years to search elsewhere for his next woman. He had only laughed at Wolfe, asking with an infuriating look if Nichelle was already taken. "You can get her anytime you want," Kingsley said. "Piss off."

With a touch of reluctance that Wolfe noticed,

Nichelle turned away from his brother. "I'll be right back, Kingsley."

With Nichelle in front of him, Wolfe suddenly didn't know what to do. Her eyes were soft tonight, the off-the-shoulder dress tempting his hands to explore the body on delectable display. He curled fingers around her arm just above the elbow and lost his breath. Her skin felt soft, so soft. He was aware of Kingsley's stare, but he didn't care.

Because he wasn't quite thinking with the head on his shoulders, Wolfe led her upstairs to his old room. He closed the door behind them.

"What's on your mind?" she asked as the lock clicked into place.

Nichelle crossed her arms and took a step back, hyper-aware of their isolation from the rest of the family. It was only her and Wolfe in his childhood room, the smell of furniture polish and old books thick around them. His *bedroom*.

"I talked to Franklin today."

She blinked in surprise. That wasn't what she'd expected him to say. Earlier that day, she'd finally made a decision about what to do with Isaac and his threats, an entire damned day devoted to that foolishness when she had more important things to do with her time. The solution she found was a workable one. It kept Quraishi and Wolfe still working together and did not leave her at Isaac's mercy as he obviously hoped.

"What was that conversation about?" Nichelle crossed her arms. "Or should I even ask?"

"It looks like you already know."

She turned away from him to sit on the wide mahogany trunk under the window, pressing her palms down into the wood on either side of her hips. "I don't like to make assumptions."

"He said you were leaving me."

She flinched. That had been part of her solution. Not an ideal one, but the only one she had been able to come up with in such a short amount of time. She'd figured Isaac would strike, but not this soon.

"Yes." She pursed her lips, wondering if she would have the courage to leave when it was time. "I am."

"What the hell?" He looked shocked. Then his face blanked, emotional walls slamming down. "How could you do this?"

"I've made the decision, and this seems to be the best thing to do. I leave Kingston Consulting, no foul."

"And take Quraishi's business with you?" His eyes narrowed, the blank look on his face leeching away to leave coldness in its place. "Are you going to sleep with him, too?"

She shot to her feet. "What did you just say to me?"

"Franklin said—" He stopped, hopefully reconsidering what he was going to say.

"No, tell me exactly what he said and what you thought I would do." She stalked to him, her high heels cracking against the hardwood floors before being muffled by the carpet near his bed. "Tell me exactly what you think I'm capable of. Tell me you don't trust me anymore."

He didn't back away from her, but his face became impossibly even colder than before. His eyes were like flint with none of the amused glimmer she was used to, even in the midst of their most ridiculous arguments.

He opened his mouth and dropped the words in the

room. Vile words. She'd said that and worse of other people, men and women, but not people she knew better of. And she would damned sure not repeat them if they weren't true.

She ignored the twisting pain in her stomach, the pressure in her chest as if someone had just shoved her to the ground and stomped on her. "And you never once questioned anything he said about me?"

"You're leaving," he said by way of an answer.

She pressed her lips together. A cry wanted to wrench free from her throat. Nichelle swallowed until the sound slid back down into her stomach and away. "You're a dick."

She fought back against him the only way she knew how. By pulling away. Wolfe wasn't like everyone else. She couldn't hurt him without hurting herself. But even this—shoving all emotion aside and emptying her face of all expression, drawing her spine tight and preparing to walk out of the room and out of his life—cracked her wide open. The back of her eyes stung. Her limbs were heavy with disappointment. With sadness.

She turned toward the door.

"Don't do that," he said, his voice deep and threatening. "Don't walk away from me."

"You don't get to make demands of me, Wolfe." She did him one better, growling low in her throat. "Not after what you just said to me. If you believe I'm the kind of parasite Isaac described, then you shouldn't want anything to do with me." She took a steadying breath and moved toward the door again. "I think we're done."

"No." He grabbed her elbow but she yanked away, gasping at the slight pain.

"Don't touch me!"

He hissed. "That's not what you said to me the other night." And there it was for the first time, his feelings in the open about what they had shared. But this was not the place, and this was not the way to do it.

"You don't get to do this to me, Wolfe. You came to *my* house with your wants."

"Tell me you didn't want me to." It was a dare.

But she couldn't say it because it wasn't true. She had wanted him so badly that it burned. Her every breath had been painful with the need of him, nothing right until she had her hands and mouth on him, their bodies twined and twisted together, heaving in the bed toward satisfaction. Wolfe stepped close, obliterating the few feet of space she had placed between them.

Clean. He smelled clean, a hint of mint toothpaste on his breath, his sandalwood aftershave.

"Tell me you don't want me now."

His confidence rubbed her raw. "I don't want you now." She threw the words defiantly at him. "And how can you even pretend to want me when you see me as nothing more than a manipulative bitch with no sense of loyalty?"

"No!" He dipped his head and kissed her.

She gasped as his open mouth touched hers, his tongue a rough inquiry, wet and instantly knee-weakening. Nichelle fisted her hands in his shirt to push him away, but ended up pulling him to her instead. Her mouth opened, releasing a gasping breath when their tongues met. They kissed as if they were starved for each other, wet and noisy and sloppy. Needful.

The sting of sudden arousal burned between her legs, and she clutched at his shoulders, moaned into the unrelenting heat of his mouth. His hands gripped her hips. Then the wall was at her back, the hard press of him at her front. She whimpered with want. The fury of earlier sloughed off to revel in the "at last" of him against her body.

Nichelle sucked on Wolfe's tongue and raked her nails under his shirt, shoving it out of the way to press her hands into the dense muscle of his stomach, his pecs. She pinched his nipples, roughly. He gasped in her mouth, pushed her harder into the wall, his hands shoving up her dress. She heard it tearing, the twenty-five-hundred-dollar Carolina Herrera sheath destroyed in the frantic heat of their lust. He ripped aside her underwear. She fumbled for his zipper, for the hard heat of him.

They came together with a thick gasp, his hands digging into her hips. Her legs locked around his waist as he slid into her again, a deep and rough claiming. She tightened her legs around him and twisted her hips, wanting more from him, more than what they had become.

He was hot and sweet and firm inside her. Her center gripped him and squeezed while her thoughts scattered beyond retrieval. His breath puffed hot against her ear. He groaned her name, like pain. Sweat shuddered to the surface of her skin, heat under her clothes while she panted and twisted, her fingernails tight in the back of his neck.

"Don't leave me!" he groaned into her neck, panting as they slammed together, fury and fear, dread and desire driving them together toward a shuddering conclusion. Her legs locked tighter around his waist. Their breaths came faster. The wall knocked with the force of his thrusts.

But—she gasped and gripped him tighter—what if someone heard them? The bed. They should move to the perfectly good bed across the room. But he shifted his grip to her buttocks, tilted the angle of his hips and slammed into her just perfectly. A screaming cry left her lips.

And she forgot all about the bed.

Her hand scrambled back, found a shelf hooked to the wall and held on as he dove up into her, slamming the delight into her again and again. They rocked against the wall, fierce and sweaty. The scent of sweat and sex, desperation and anger and heat rose up like steam. Pleasure scraped her raw, twisting in her middle, gripping her so hard that she gasped his name, raked her nails down his sides. He hissed but did not stop the relentless work of his hips.

He clutched the back of her neck, forcing her head back. He showed his teeth, his canines bared, sweat dripping down his face.

"Don't. Leave. Me." He punctuated each word with a pump of his hips. "Please. Stay. Don't—" The words fell away into scattered curses. His eyes squeezed shut as his orgasm felled him. She felt the heated spurt of him between her thighs, and was then racing to catch up with him. A breathless moment later, she was shuddering, too, and crying out into the soaked collar of his shirt.

They trembled against each other, falling as one from the height they'd achieved together.

"Wolfe…" His name shuddered from her lips when her feet touched the ground.

Nichelle staggered on her high heels, panting and holding on to the wall with trembling fingers. She was slippery and hot under her clothes, between her legs. What had she done? She stared at Wolfe. He stumbled back from her, looking as shocked and breathless as she felt. He shoved himself back into his pants, looking anywhere but at her.

Nichelle yanked down her dress, feeling every bit the fool, even more than last time. His trust was just as important to her as his love. The fact that he didn't trust her anymore and could take the word of some nobody over what they'd shared for most of their lives made her sick to her stomach. She searched for the right words. "I'll leave the partnership dissolution papers on your desk tonight for you to sign. I won't be back in the office tomorrow." Those words weren't exactly right, but they would have to do.

Wolfe stumbled toward her. "No. Nichelle. Please."

She evaded his touch. "You already said enough." Nichelle left the room, head high, with as much of her dignity as she had left. Behind her, she heard him begin to follow, but she slipped quickly down the hallway and into a guest bathroom to tidy up.

When she was presentable, she snuck out the back door, sending Nala a text when she was in her car, but telling no one else she was leaving. She'd leave it up to Wolfe if he felt like giving explanations. This…thing… they had was over. She couldn't do this anymore. And she meant it this time. There were only so many times she would break her heart for a man.

Even this one.

Chapter 12

Nichelle walked out on the balcony of her rented condo and into the lush heat of a late-summer San Diego. She held the phone to her ear, humming in response to what her sister, Madalie, was saying.

It had been three weeks since she'd left Florida. She hadn't answered a single phone call from anyone at Kingston or from Wolfe's family. Everything she needed to do for the firm she'd done the night before she left for the airport. She'd cut the ties so effectively that she left herself bleeding, too. It hurt.

Nichelle leaned her forearms against the balcony and stared down at the narrow road below and the sandy beach beyond it. At barely two on a Thursday afternoon, there was already a decent amount of people on the beach, many sunning themselves, along with a few swimmers.

"Are you ever coming back?" Madalie asked the same question Nichelle had asked herself nearly every day she'd been in California. Her sister sounded sad over the phone, heartbreakingly so.

"I don't know." Nichelle gave the non-answer with a suffocating heaviness in her chest. "There are just some things I need to work out."

"With Wolfe, right?"

She sucked on the inside of her lip and ignored the abrupt dip in her stomach at the mention of his name. "Yes," she admitted. The afternoon sun pressed soft kisses into her cheek and her throat, while a delicate breeze teased the back of her neck. Although she ached deeply, the weather soothed her in small ways.

"Wolfe is here in Miami. You can't work things out with him if you're all the way over there." Her sister's voice cracked. "We miss you."

Nichelle pressed a fist to her forehead and squinted into the sun. Was she being selfish by running away? "I miss you guys, too, Maddie. I'll be home as soon as I can."

Her sister's watery sigh came loudly through the phone. "Okay."

A sudden knock on her door dragged her attention from her sister's suspiciously thick breathing. Madalie had always been the more independent of her sisters, but she was also the one who felt things the most keenly. "There's someone at the door, Maddie. I have to go."

"Okay, okay. Just come home soon. Okay? Bye." The line went silent.

Nichelle sighed. *Dammit.* At the door, she put her eye to the peephole. A man's tie appeared, something conservative and expensive. She swallowed thickly for a moment before she realized there was no way it could be Wolfe. He wouldn't wear a suit and tie in the heat of San Diego. And he would never follow her to California, even if he knew where she was.

But the man on her doorstep still surprised her.

"Garrison." Wolfe's best friend. "What are you doing here?"

"Visiting you." He gave her one of his restrained smiles, his eyes warming long before his mouth curled up ever so faintly at the corners.

Garrison and Wolfe were the opposite of the other. Wolfe was outgoing and charming, dropping panties with a simple glance while Garrison was more reserved, his looks not exactly magazine-worthy. But there was a restrained heat to him, a subtle sensuality and masculine presence. His new wife had discovered, to her contentment, just how much of a prize he was while the women who'd blown him off in college in favor of chasing the flashier and much more in-demand Wolfe were now crying into their martinis.

"Come in." She welcomed him into the condo with a wave.

He stepped past her with the faint scent of coffee and something else she couldn't identify. "I'm here because you're not answering Wolfe's calls."

Another thing she liked about Garrison, he was always upfront. You never had to guess where he stood.

"There's a reason I'm not answering his calls," she muttered, leading him into the brightly lit living room. "I don't want to talk to him."

"I gathered that much," he said dryly.

In the kitchen, she poured him a glass of sweet tea

without asking, took a glass of water for herself and sat down on the couch across from him.

"He's a wreck over what's happened between the two of you," Garrison said.

"Why is everything always about him?" She tightened her lips. "He said things to me that I never thought would come from his mouth." She arched an eyebrow at him. "Did he tell you that?"

"Yes. He did."

She swallowed in surprise. "Then he knows nothing can be done to fix it. There was no point in sending you—"

"He didn't send me."

This time she couldn't hide her surprise. Garrison, looking debonair and elegant in his pale blue summer-weight suit, crossed one knee over the other.

"Wolfe feels guilty about the things he said, like he deserves to be punished. He knows you better than some subpar tactician with severe talent envy." Nichelle almost smiled at his description of Isaac Franklin. "He's sorry but won't come to you because he's got his metaphoric hair shirt on and is rolling around in it all over Miami. And New York, too, incidentally."

"Good for him." She sneered.

"Nichelle."

"Yes?"

"Forgive him." The faintest hint of a plea crept into his tone.

"I can't. Why should I?"

"He loves you."

"He's got a real nice way of showing it." She drew a painful breath. Everything she'd forced herself to forget in Miami rushed back to her with each word Garrison uttered. It was beyond agony.

"All I'm asking is for you to give him a chance. Answer his call next time. Be open to hearing what he has to say."

"I won't make any promises, Garrison." She bit her lip, crumbling into the sofa, her superwoman facade fading away. "It's been *so* damn hard." Her voice trembled, and she gripped her hands in her lap.

"Jesus." He looked abruptly uncomfortable. But he sank into the seat next to her and settled a hand on her forearm.

"Stop torturing each other with this separation." He squeezed her arm. "Just talk to him."

Tears tickled the back of Nichelle's throat. Her body felt hot and miserable with unhappiness. But it was better than opening herself to be hurt by Wolfe again. He was to blame for what happened this time. But if she allowed him back in, she would be to blame for the resulting heartache.

Nichelle swallowed her tears and looked Garrison full in the face. "Tell him to go screw himself."

Only once he was gone did she allow the tears to run like acid down her face.

Before Garrison came, she had been having a decent week. Never one to wallow in anything, especially not her feelings, she dove into re-establishing her West Coast business connections and plunged into the cool water of the Pacific to wear herself out to the point of exhaustion when that work didn't distract her enough.

But with Wolfe's best friend came doubts about the choices she'd made. Three days after Garrison left, she still couldn't stop thinking about his visit. She reached out to her business contacts, working toward making her relocation to California a permanent thing. But after the phone calls and emails were done, her mind raced back to Garrison and the conversation they'd had.

Wolfe was miserable. He loved her. But not enough to make the journey to California himself. He'd told Garrison everything. But he didn't trust Nichelle. She prowled the condo, only a breath away from tears.

Just stop thinking about him!

Close to sunset, she pulled the front door shut behind her with keys, cash and phone in her jeans pocket. She couldn't stay in the condo any longer. After wandering the neighborhood for nearly an hour, she ended up at the little corner store near the head shop on Mission Boulevard.

The bell over the door jangled as she walked in.

"Ms. Wright." The man behind the counter, more of a boy really, greeted her with his eager smile.

"Hey, Raj."

She already visited the little store too often. Since leaving Miami, she'd developed an aversion to grocery stores, especially the big, bright ones. They left her feeling exposed and alone, waiting for something that would never come. But Raj's corner store with its constant supply of overpriced condiments and pasta and coffee was perfect.

"Things going all right today?" She chatted with him as usual since he seemed always happy to see her, a boy with a crush, which was sweet and helped scrape some of her ego off the ground.

"Yes, ma'am." His face was handsome and eager behind the glass partition. When she looked away in her search for her favorite Ben and Jerry's ice cream, she sensed his eyes on her. She found the Chunky Monkey and took it up to the window to pay.

"Another one, huh?"

She nodded, refusing to get embarrassed about her sadness addiction. Five pints in three weeks. It was a good thing she got up to swim every morning; otherwise she wouldn't be able to fit into her suits by the time she found a new job.

"Just a little something to tide me over until dinner," she said, not sure she was entirely joking.

"It's a delicious flavor," the boy said. "You have good taste." He dipped his head, subtle color touching his cheeks.

"Thank you, Raj." She gave him a smile of her own, then collected her change. "See you next time."

"See you!"

Nichelle swung the plastic bag with the ice cream at her side as she left the corner store and its ringing bell behind. She stepped out in the sunlight and bumped into the person standing near the doorway.

"Excuse me," she said.

"No need to be excused," came a familiar voice. "It was my fault."

She jumped away from the steadying hands, her heart pounding frantically in her chest. Wolfe frowned down at her from his looming height. At least she thought it was Wolfe. This version of him was fully bearded with a thick fuzz of hair on his head and new lines around his mouth. Instead of a suit, he wore black Converse, faded jeans and a plain black T-shirt. Sunglasses shaded his eyes.

She gasped softly at the change in him, because yes,

it was him. With that single touch on her arms, the scent of him, the brief crush of his broad chest against her, she knew immediately who it was.

She looked around the street, expecting to see Garrison meandering someplace nearby. Despite the runaway pace of her heartbeat, she pulled herself together and took another step back.

"Was Garrison supposed to soften me up for the kill?" She gripped the plastic bag with the ice cream against her belly, grateful for the cold, grounding pressure of it on her skin.

"What?" Frown lines etched into Wolfe's brow.

"Don't play stupid with me. I told Garrison I didn't want to see you. You can take your bad feelings and shove them up your—"

"Garrison was here?"

"You didn't send him?"

His frown deepened. "Why would I?"

Truthfully, sending an emissary didn't seem like Wolfe's style. If he wanted to deal with a problem, he usually confronted it head on, despite any possible consequences.

"It doesn't matter anyway." She gave him a dismissive glance. "You wasted your time coming out here."

"It's not wasted since I got to see you."

She rolled her eyes. "Enough with the bull."

"This is no bull, Nichelle." He crossed his arms over his chest, both a protective and vulnerable gesture. "I needed to see you."

"And what, it took you three weeks to get your courage up?"

He looked away, eyes skittering over the storefronts nearby, the awning of the corner store, the pretty girl who walked past in her bikini and UGG boots. His forehead wrinkled in confusion when he looked again at the girl, and Nichelle almost smiled.

"It's a California thing," she said. She stepped past him to wait for the light to cross the busy street. He kept up with her. "Why are you following me?"

"I want to talk with you."

"We already said enough the last time we saw each other."

"No, we didn't. I—"

Nichelle stepped out into the street before the light changed. She couldn't listen to another word. She didn't want to hear his excuses for ripping her heart out of her chest and stomping it to pieces under his designer Italian shoes.

A car horn honked. Tires screamed.

Wolfe yanked her out of the street moments before a car plowed through the intersection. His arms lashed tight over her belly, painful and protective. She cried out, frightened, and dropped the ice cream. It rolled into the street. Another car sped through the green light and crushed the carton. Nichelle stared in horror at the pulverized carton still mostly encased in white plastic, banana ice cream and walnuts exploding from the bag and already melting on the street.

"Dammit, I didn't come here for you to kill yourself!"

Wolfe didn't let go. His heart thudded hard against her shoulder blade. But her heartbeat wasn't any calmer. When the crosswalk light changed, Wolfe tugged her across the street toward the narrow path heading down to the beach. Nichelle pressed a hand to her chest, willing herself to calm down. She wiped a hand through the cold sweat on her forehead.

"I'm sorry," she said after her heart stopped racing. "That was stupid of me."

"It *was* stupid." Wolfe tucked her under his arm and fumbled a kiss to her jaw. "But I've done my share of stupid, too."

She bit her lip and relaxed into his embrace, into the sweat-flavored solidity of him. The day was bright with sun, heat pulsing around them, the afternoon wavering like a mirage. Nichelle briefly closed her eyes. Was all of this some crazy dream? Would she wake up in her condo, crying out in grief and loss like she had so many times before?

A pack of giggling girls walking toward them nudged each other, staring at Wolfe, then at her. Their envious looks made her feel self-conscious. She pulled away from Wolfe, although immediately she wanted to curl into him again.

He quietly released her. They walked through the clutter of bikini- and shorts-clad teenagers. It was a Sunday. No school and a packed Mission Beach. Instead of leading her toward her condo, Wolfe steered her with a gentle nudge of his shoulder away from the path toward her place and down to the water.

He paused to toe off his shoes and carry them while she trudged along at his side in the sand. The beach was crowded, mostly surfers and sunbathers, some families with their laughing children, ridiculously beautiful people playing beach volleyball nearby in little more than their underwear.

Nichelle found a quiet spot on the hot sand and sat down. Wolfe settled next to her. She took off her shoes, crossed her arms and balanced her chin on her bent knees, staring out into the water.

"You should go," she said.

"I can't." There was nothing melodramatic in his words, simply a statement of fact. "My mother will kill me if I come back to Miami without you."

"I'm sure you'll manage to recover."

He shifted at her side, his linked arms curved around his bent knees. He stared out at the water, sunlight glinting off his shades. "Nichelle. I was an idiot."

"You've always been an idiot."

A huff of sound, amusement and exasperation, left his mouth. Nichelle bit her lip again. Something about the relaxed ease of him on the sand beside her, the firm warmth of his arm against hers, the pounding of the surf, reminded her how much she'd thought of them like this, lying on the beach in Miami. Just the two of them without any worries. None of his women. No work. Just them and the sun and the weight of their feelings between them. The memory weakened her.

She sighed and dropped down into the sand, lying on her back. He lay with her, tucking his arms behind his head. His big body heaved with a sigh of its own.

"I love you."

She tensed at the unexpected declaration. "You don't accuse someone you love of betraying you. Especially when you know it's not true."

"I *did* know you would never do that to me. Can't I use my rampant jealousy as an excuse?" She heard the faint humor in his voice, the attempt at teasing.

"As if I could ever sleep with Isaac Franklin. He's weak." *And he's not you.*

Wolfe choked on a laughing breath, then stilled. "He

talked about your mole. The one here." He touched her through the jeans. "I just saw red. But instead of taking it out on him, I let my paranoia do the damage." He cursed softly. "I'm sorry. I knew better and I'm sorry."

"You know that anyone who's seen me in a bikini has seen that mole, right?"

"Hell! I know…" His voice faded away. "Once I pulled my head out of my ass, I realized that. Sorry doesn't begin to cover what I feel."

"And you think that should change things back to how they were between us?"

"No, I don't." He rolled to face her in the sand.

Bright sunlight reflected off the gold in his sunglasses. She squinted against the glare. After a brief pause, he took off the glasses. And she saw what he'd been trying to hide, the heavy sorrow in his eyes. "I don't want things to go back to how they were," he said. "I want them to be better." He took another breath. "I want…"

For the first time in her adult life, Nichelle saw Wolfe hesitate. He licked his lips, and her eyes grew wider. He was nervous. His hand moved between their bodies, brushing her hip, then her belly. Then his hand emerged with a familiar scarlet box. "I want you to wear this again, but for real this time."

A breath stuttered from her. "What is that?" But her body already knew what it was. She grew warm, happiness heating her from the inside out. Wolfe opened the box, and the canary diamonds winked at her in the sunlight.

"This is an inadequate symbol of my love and trust," he said. "I love you. I trust you, and I can't allow myself to forget that again. This is my promise to you that I won't."

She swallowed. "You don't need to marry me just to keep me in Miami, Wolfe."

"Does that mean you'll come back to me? I want to marry you to keep you in my bed and in my life. I want to make official what everyone's been saying about us for years. And I want to prove to you that I'm worthy of the trust and love you give me every day."

She bit her lip to stifle a smile. "I never said I love you."

His mouth tilted. "You don't have to say it." He took the engagement ring out of the box. "So, will you?"

Yes. Yes! "I'll think about it," she said. "I'm surprised you haven't assumed my answer since you apparently know me so well."

"I have. But I'm giving you the courtesy of allowing you to say it out loud."

She took the ring from him and slid it into her pocket. "Ask me again when we're back home."

A shudder ran through his body, a hiss of relief. He wasn't as confident as he claimed. "God, yes."

She smiled at the vulnerability in his face, the easing of the tightness around his eyes, the way his beautiful mouth softened. His tongue brushed over his full lower lip.

"Nichelle." There was a pleading in his voice.

"Wolfe." And because she knew the man she would soon marry, knew what he needed, she whispered the three words in his ear.

"Then kiss me," he said.

And she did. The press of their mouths together was a sweet welcome that soon became a heated slide of tongue and lips, hands pushing under T-shirts to find warm skin. An embarrassing sound leaked from her mouth, need and relief. Wolfe's fingers curved around her ribs, a thumb stroking the underside of her breast.

Something smacked into Nichelle's leg. She gasped, jerking back.

"Sorry! Sorry!" A slim girl in a bikini grabbed a volleyball near Nichelle's feet, then ran off across the sand.

Wolfe laughed and stood up, the corners of his eyes crinkling with happiness. "We should continue this conversation someplace private, don't you think?" He reached down to help her to her feet.

Nichelle put a hand in his, and he tugged her up into his arms. "Yes," she murmured, a smile as wide as the whole ocean spreading across her face. "We should."

She pressed close to Wolfe and buried her face in his chest, drawing in a deep breath of him that was like home. A place she'd been all along.

Epilogue

"Is she pregnant?"

Wolfe, who'd been buttoning his shirt while his mother's voice blared from the speaker of his cell, grabbed the phone off the bed. He took it off speaker. "What?!"

His mother laughed at his outrage. "Did you knock Nichelle up before the wedding? Is that why you had a quick ceremony on our back lawn less than a week after bringing her back from California?"

Although his mother couldn't see, Wolfe shook his head. He darted a glance toward the closed bathroom door of their hotel and stepped away. He didn't want Nichelle to hear the crazy things his mother was saying. The music of Paris, church bells and faint conversation from a café nearby hummed at him through the open window.

He and Nichelle had arrived in France three hours before, jet-lagged from the journey. But instead of falling into the bed to sleep, they had fallen on each other, passionate and eager to make love for the first time as man and wife.

Nichelle, with laughter in her voice, had asked him several times on the long flight why he'd booked the tickets for immediately after the wedding, knowing they had a nine-hour flight ahead of them and no chance for a true wedding night. But he hadn't been thinking about that when he made the arrangements. He just wanted to finally start the life with her he'd imagined for so long.

So, no. Nichelle wasn't pregnant. But it wasn't for lack of trying.

"Mama, the rush was all mine. But it has nothing to do with a surprise baby."

"If you say so." The sound of a door slamming came to him through the phone. "Get on with your honeymooning then. Thanks for letting us know you arrived safely, although I'm sure you got in long before now."

His neck heated again, but he refused to rise to the bait. "You're welcome."

"I'll tell your father to stop planning for his first grandchild. Too bad, he was getting excited. And I was, too, to tell the truth."

"Mama, I'll talk with you later."

"Yes, my son. Enjoy Paris and your new wife."

He disconnected the call and rubbed the back of his neck. Nichelle carrying his child. The thought warmed him, made him eager to take her to bed again and make it a reality.

"Did I hear something about me being knocked up?"

His wife emerged from the bathroom, flawless in a

royal blue dress and black high heels, mouth red with lipstick. She smelled of the shower and a light citrus perfume, and had changed from the leggings and sweater she'd worn on the plane, or rather the leggings and shirt he'd torn off her as soon as the hotel room door shut. Nichelle was his *wife*. The canary diamond rings once again on her finger proved it. The quick ceremony in his parents' backyard cemented it. And now they were in Paris on their honeymoon, in the place where it all started.

"Yes." Wolfe drew her into his arms. "She thinks I shamefully knocked you up, and that's the reason I ran off to France with you so quickly. My brothers have a bet going, apparently. I told her whoever started that bet had already lost."

The corner of Nichelle's red mouth tilted up in an odd smile. She slid her arms around his neck, sweet breath and sweeter body stirring him all over again. "Well, maybe not."

Wolfe froze, the shock of her declaration tightening his spine. "Do you mean to say…?" He couldn't go on. He stood still in the perfumed sanctuary of her arms, his body torn in two directions as she bit his earlobe and slid her palms over his chest through the half-buttoned shirt.

"No need to tell them now, though," she murmured.

"When—when did this happen?"

"The night before I left for California, I'm guessing." She licked his ear, and he felt the smiling curve of her mouth against his throat. He pulled carefully away to stare down at his wife, soon to be the mother of his child. "Should we even be…?" *Making love?* The shock of her revelation apparently rendered him incapable of finishing a sentence.

Nichelle crossed her arms. "If I thought you'd treat me like spun glass, I wouldn't have told you until we got home." She pursed her lips. "I'm not delicate, Wolfe, just pregnant. And only a little pregnant at that." Then she smiled, dropping her gaze.

Wolfe's heart tripped in his chest at the utter vulnerability on her face. *Jesus.* "Nichelle…" He dropped to his knees and pressed his ear to her flat stomach. "I love you more and more every day."

"Hopefully not because I'm about to add another Diallo to the world." She stroked his face. "Get off your knees, husband of mine. There will be plenty of time for that later. If memory serves, you promised me some French food and music this afternoon."

Wolfe stood up. "You're incredible. You know that?"

"Of course. And you're my well-deserved prize." She smiled up into his eyes and looped her arms around his waist. "I was going to wait until we got back home to tell you about the baby, but…" She shrugged, looking uncharacteristically shy. "As usual, your mother forced my hand."

Wolfe groaned as something suddenly occurred to him. "She's going to think that I lied to her."

"No, she won't. I'll tell her the truth."

The truth that he was going to be a father. A *father.* Wolfe barely knew what to do. He'd made plans for them for the day. But now that he had a child on the way…

"Stop. Stop whatever foolishness you're thinking right now." She laughed at him, dragged him close again and kissed him quickly on the mouth. Her fingers fastened the remaining buttons on his shirt. "Are you ready?"

Earlier they had decided that to increase the likelihood of them getting out of the hotel room that afternoon, they would shower separately. Wolfe went first, taking his twenty minutes in the bathroom before making way for Nichelle to luxuriate under the hot spray and come out of the bathroom looking as if she was on the way to a fashion show.

"Yes." He kissed the corners of her mouth, the tip of her nose. "I've been ready for you forever."

"My charming husband."

They left the room, Nichelle in the protective crook of his arm, the sweet weight of her against him making Wolfe feel lucky with every step.

"*Monsieur* Diallo." The hotel concierge signaled to him as they passed through the lobby. "This arrived for you today." She passed him an envelope. It was eggshell white and thick, expensive paper that smelled faintly of incense.

"Thank you."

Wolfe wondered briefly what was in the envelope. Only Nala, Wolfe's parents and secretary knew exactly where he and Nichelle were. No one else had been told the specifics of their trip.

"What's that?"

"No idea." He turned the envelope over in his hands, then stepped with Nichelle out into the sunny afternoon.

"Open it. Do you think someone sent us a present?"

He chuckled at her childlike excitement, reminded again of the actual child in her belly. His fingers drifted to her stomach. She leaned into his caress, smiling. "Who knew you were such a softie for babies?"

"Definitely not me." He'd only considered children in the abstract before, and only in the context of his promise to provide at least one grandchild to his parents. "But now…"

"Now you're the most excited daddy-to-be there ever was."

And the sparkle and flash in her eyes told him that Nichelle might be the most excited mommy-to-be there ever was. To satisfy her curiosity about the envelope, he paused on the front steps of the hotel to open it. As expected, it was a card.

On the occasion of your wedding.

"Another wedding card for us." Although it was addressed to Wolfe alone.

"But why did they send it here?" she asked. "Is it from our parents?"

Congratulations on making an honest woman out of Mademoiselle Wright. On your way back from Paris, consider a stop in Essaouira with my compliments. May you experience even more joy in your life together. With your partnership secured, I look forward to a long and fruitful relationship with Kingston Consulting.
Best,
Jamal al Din Quraishi

The smile dropped from Wolfe's face.

Nichelle's attention had already wandered from the card to the cobblestoned streets and the beautiful city around them. She walked ahead of him, heels delicately tapping the cobblestones with each step. Her hip-rock-ing stroll drew his eyes, the way the red-soled shoes elongated her legs, flexed the muscles in her calves and made her firm and round bottom even more of a miracle. He no longer had to pretend he wasn't looking. Nichelle walked with the loose stride of a confident and happy woman. She peeked over her shoulder at him, wearing that smile that curled desire in his belly, love in his heart. She clasped her hands behind her, bringing his eyes low to the fire flash of the yellow diamonds on her finger and the full curve of her bottom in the peacock-blue dress. She crooked a finger at him: *Come here.*

"What's distracting you from me?" she asked when he caught up to her.

"The card is from Quraishi. He wishes us well."

"Does he?" She looked surprised. But there was something else, too.

"What am I missing?" he asked.

Nichelle worried her lower lip between her teeth, then put a hand over his heart. "Before I left for California, I told Quraishi the truth. I told him our marriage deception was my idea and that I'd resigned from the company. I assured him that Kingston Consulting would still take excellent care of his business interests."

This smaller shock only rocked Wolfe back on his heels a little. "But he never said anything to me. He never asked to nullify the contract. Nothing."

"That's good." Her mouth twitched, a tiny smile of triumph. "I tried to make sure you wouldn't have to deal with the fallout. I guess it worked."

After Nichelle had left for California, Quraishi said nothing to him about dissolving the partnership or even about Nichelle being with the company. The man had simply carried on with their business arrangement as if nothing had changed. Except for a cryptic email in which he'd said he hoped to hear from Nichelle again soon, everything was the same. At the time, Wolfe had been too worried about getting Nichelle back to his side that he hadn't thought much about his business. But it all made sense now.

Nichelle had shielded him with her love yet again. He felt once more the familiar twinge of anger at himself, the regret that he'd allowed doubt to come between them and fool him into thinking she wasn't worthy of his trust.

She dug her fingers gently into his chest through his shirt. A warning. "It's in the past now," she said. "We have the future to look forward to. Together."

Nichelle was right. Still, he'd make up his lapse to her somehow. For now...

"Mrs. Nichelle Wright-Diallo, would you do me the honor of accompanying me to a concert this afternoon?" He smiled down at her, willing all the love he had for her to show on his face.

Faint color moved under her cheeks. "Of course, husband."

Wolfc linked his fingers with hers and they turned as one, walking side by side toward a future they had always shared.

* * * * *

From their first kiss…

It's ONLY You

SHERYL LISTER

Record label VP Donovan Wright saves ER nurse Simona Andrews's life, and she promptly declares she won't date him. Donovan is a media darling, and since she became her niece's guardian, Simona wants to avoid high-profile affairs. Yet Donovan's touch sets her on fire. Before she walks away for good, he has one chance to prove that his promise to love her will never be broken…

Available September 2015!

REQUEST YOUR FREE BOOKS!

2 FREE NOVELS
PLUS 2 FREE GIFTS!

KIMANI™ ROMANCE

Love's ultimate destination!